Opening the door, Letty gasped.

Darius stood in her doorway, dressed in a black button-down shirt with well-cut jeans that showed the rugged lines of his powerful body. It was barely noon, but his jaw was dark with a five-o'clock shadow.

For a moment, even hating and fearing him as she did, Letty was dazzled by that ruthless masculine beauty.

"Letty," he greeted her coldly. Then his eyes dropped to her baby bump.

With an intake of breath, Letty tried to shut the door in his face.

He blocked her with his powerful shoulder and pushed his way into her apartment.

"So it's true," he said in a low voice. "You're pregnant."

She looked frozen. Then she squared her shoulders, tossing her dark ponytail in a futile gesture of bravado. "So?"

"Is the baby mine?"

"Yours?" Her eyes shot sparks of fire, even though she had dark shadows beneath, as if she hadn't been sleeping well. "What makes you think the baby's yours? Maybe I slept with ten men since our night. Maybe I slept with a hundred—"

"You're lying."

One Night With Consequences

When one night...leads to pregnancy!

When succumbing to a night of unbridled desire, it's impossible to think past the morning after!

But with the sheets barely settled, that little blue line appears on the pregnancy test and it doesn't take long to realize that one night of white-hot passion has turned into a lifetime of consequences!

Only one question remains:

How do you tell a man you've just met that you're about to share more than just his bed?

Find out in:

Look for more **One Night With Consequences** coming soon!

Jennie Lucas

——

THE CONSEQUENCE OF HIS VENGEANCE

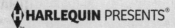

HARLEQUIN PRESENTS®

Recycling programs
for this product may
not exist in your area.

ISBN-13: 978-0-373-21312-2

The Consequence of His Vengeance

First North American publication 2017

Copyright © 2017 by Jennie Lucas

Printed in U.S.A.

USA TODAY bestselling author **Jennie Lucas**'s parents owned a bookstore, and she grew up surrounded by books, dreaming about faraway lands. A fourth-generation Westerner, she went east at sixteen to boarding school on scholarship, wandered the world, got married, then finally worked her way through college before happily returning to her hometown. A 2010 RITA® Award finalist and 2005 Golden Heart® Award winner, she lives in Idaho with her husband and children.

Books by Jennie Lucas

Harlequin Presents

Uncovering Her Nine Month Secret
The Sheikh's Last Seduction
To Love, Honor and Betray
A Night of Living Dangerously
The Virgin's Choice
Bought: The Greek's Baby

Wedlocked!

Baby of His Revenge

One Night With Consequences

A Ring for Vincenzo's Heir
Nine Months to Redeem Him

At His Service

The Consequences of That Night

Princes Untamed

Dealing Her Final Card
A Reputation for Revenge

One Night In...

Reckless Night in Rio

Visit the Author Profile page at Harlequin.com for more titles.

To Pippa Roscoe, with best wishes for a brilliant future. You are going to rock it!

CHAPTER ONE

LETTY SPENCER HUNCHED her shoulders against the frosty February night as she pushed out of the Brooklyn diner, door swinging behind her. Her body was exhausted after her double shift, but not half as weary as her heart.

It had not been a good day.

Shivering in her threadbare coat, Letty lowered her head against the biting wind on the dark street. Snow flurries brushed against her exposed skin.

"Letitia." The voice was low and husky behind her. Letty's back snapped straight.

No one called her Letitia anymore, not even her father. Letitia Spencer had been the pampered heiress of Fairholme. Letty was just another New York waitress struggling to make ends meet for her family.

And that voice sounded like...

He sounded like...

Gripping her purse strap tight, she slowly turned around.

And lost her breath.

Darius Kyrillos stood against a glossy black sports car parked on the street. Dark-haired and dark-eyed, he was devastatingly handsome and powerful in his well-cut suit and black wool coat, standing beneath the softly falling snowflakes illuminated by a streetlight.

For a moment, Letty struggled to make sense of what her eyes were telling her. Darius? Here?

"Did you see this?" her father had said excitedly that morning, spreading the newspaper across their tiny kitchen counter. "Darius Kyrillos sold his company for twenty billion dollars!" He looked up, his eyes unfocused with painkillers, his recently broken arm awkward in a sling. "You should call him, Letty. Make him love you again."

After ten years, her father had said Darius's name out loud. He'd broken the unspoken rule. She'd fled, mumbling that she'd be late for work.

But it had affected her all day, making her clumsily drop trays and forget orders. She'd even dumped a plate of eggs and bacon on a customer. It was a miracle she hadn't been fired.

No, Letty thought, unable to breathe. This was the miracle. Right now.

Darius.

She took a step toward him on the sidewalk, her eyes wide.

"Darius?" she whispered. "Is it really you?"

He came forward like a dark angel. She could see his breath beneath the streetlight like white smoke in the icy night. He stopped, towering over her. The light frosted his dark hair, leaving his face in shadow. She half expected him to disappear if she tried to touch him. So she didn't.

Then he touched her.

Reaching out, he stroked a dark tendril that had escaped her ponytail, twisted it around his finger. "You're surprised?"

At the sound of that low, husky voice, lightly accented from his early childhood in Greece, a deep shiver sent a rush of prickles over her skin. And she knew he wasn't a dream.

Her heart pounded. Darius. The man she'd tried not to crave for the last decade. The man she'd dreamed about against her will, night after night. Here. Now. She choked out a sob. "What are you doing here?"

His dark eyes ran over her hungrily. "I couldn't resist."

As he moved his head, the streetlight illuminated his face. He hadn't changed at all, Letty thought in wonder. The same years that had nearly destroyed her hadn't touched him. He was the same man she remembered, the one she'd once loved with all her innocent heart, back when she'd been a headstrong eighteen-year-old, caught up in a forbidden love affair. Before she'd sacrificed her own happiness to save his.

His hand moved down to her shoulder. Feeling his warmth through her thin coat, she wanted to cry, to ask him what had taken so long. She'd almost given up hope.

Then she saw his gaze linger on her old coat, with its broken zipper, and her diner uniform, a white dress that had been bleached so many times it was starting to fray. Usually, she also wore unfashionable nylons to keep her legs warm while she was on her feet all day in white orthopedic shoes. But today, her last pair had been unwearable with too many rips, so her legs were bare.

Following his gaze, she blushed. "I'm not really dressed for going out…"

"Your clothes don't matter." There was a strange undercurrent in his voice. "Let's go."

"Go? Where?"

He took her hand in his own, palm to palm, and she suddenly didn't feel the snowflakes or cold. Waves of electricity scattered helter-skelter across her body, across her skin, from her scalp to her toes.

"My penthouse. In Midtown." He looked down at her. "Will you come?"

"Yes," she breathed.

His sensual lips curved oddly before he led her to his shiny, low-slung sports car and opened the passenger door.

As Letty climbed in, she took a deep breath, inhaling the scent of rich leather. This car likely cost more than she'd earned the past decade waiting tables. She moved her hand along the fine calfskin, the color of pale cream. She'd forgotten leather could be so soft.

Climbing in beside her, Darius started the engine. The car roared away from the curb, humming through the night, leaving her neighborhood to travel through the gentrified areas of Park Slope and Brooklyn Heights before finally crossing the Manhattan Bridge into the New York borough that most catered to tourists and the wealthy: Manhattan.

All the while, Letty was intensely aware of him beside her. Her gaze fell upon his hand and thick wrist, laced with dark hair, as he changed gears.

"So." His voice was ironic. "Your father is out of prison."

Biting her lip, she looked at him hesitantly beneath her lashes. "A few days ago."

Darius glanced back at her old coat and fraying uniform. "And now you're ready to change your life."

Was that a question or a suggestion? Did he mean that *he* wanted to change it? Had he actually learned the truth about why she'd betrayed him ten years ago?

"I've learned the hard way," she said in a low voice, "that life changes, whether you're ready or not."

His hands tightened as he turned back to the steering wheel. "True."

Letty's eyes lingered on his profile, from the dark slash of eyebrows to his aquiline nose and full, sensual mouth. She still felt like she was dreaming. *Darius Kyrillos.* After all these years, he'd found her at the diner and was whisking her off to his penthouse. The only man she'd ever truly loved...

"Why did you come for me?" she whispered. "Why today, after all these years?"

His dark gaze was veiled. "Your message."

She hadn't sent any message. "What message?"

"Fine," he murmured, baring his teeth in a smile. "Have it your way."

Message? Letty felt a skitter of dark suspicion. Her father had wanted her to contact Darius. For the last few days, since he'd broken his arm in mysterious circumstances he wouldn't explain, he'd been home on painkillers, sitting next to her ancient computer with nothing to do.

Could her father have sent Darius a message, pretending to be her?

She glanced at Darius, then decided she didn't care. If her father had interfered, all she could be was grateful, if this was the result.

Her father must have revealed her real reasons for betraying Darius ten years ago. She couldn't imagine he would even be talking to her now otherwise.

But how to know for sure?

Biting her lip, she said awkwardly, "I read about you in the paper this morning. That you sold. Your company, I mean."

"Ah." His jaw set as he turned away. "Right."

His voice was cold. No wonder, Letty thought. She sounded like an idiot. She tried to steady herself. "Congratulations."

"Thank you. It cost ten years of my life."

Ten years. Those two simple words hung between them in silence, like a small raft on an ocean of regret.

Their car entered Manhattan, with all its wealth and savagery. A place she'd avoided since her father's trial and sentencing almost a decade before.

Her heartbeat fluttered in her throat as she looked down at her chapped hands, folded tightly in her lap. "I've thought of you a lot, wondering how you were. Hoping you were well. Hoping you were happy."

Stopping at a red light, Darius abruptly looked at her.

"It was good of you to think of me," he drawled in a low voice, once again with that strange undercurrent. In the cold night of the city, headlights of passing cars moved shadows across the hard lines of his face.

The light changed to green. It was just past ten o'clock, and the traffic was starting to lessen. Heading north on First Avenue, they passed the United Nations plaza. The buildings had started climbing higher against the sky as they approached Midtown. Turning off Forty-Ninth onto the gracious width of Park Avenue, they approached a newly built glass-and-steel skyscraper on the south side of Central Park.

As he pulled his car into the porte cochere, she was craning her neck back in astonishment. "You live here?"

"I have the top two floors," he said casually, in the way someone might say, *I have tickets to the ballet.*

His door opened, and he handed the keys to a smiling valet who greeted him respectfully by name. Coming around, Darius opened Letty's door. He held out his hand.

She stared at it nervously, then put her hand in his.

He wrapped it tightly in his own. She felt the warmth and roughness of his palm against hers.

He had to know, she thought desperately. He had to. Otherwise, why would he have sought her out? Why wouldn't he still hate her?

He led her through the awe-inspiring lobby, with its minimalist furniture and twenty-foot ceilings.

"Good evening, Mr. Kyrillos," the man at the desk said. "Cold weather we're having. Hope you're staying warm!"

Darius held Letty's hand tightly. She felt like she might catch flame as he drew her across the elegant, cavernous lobby. "I am. Thank you, Perry."

He waved his key fob in front of the elevator's wall panel and pressed the seventieth floor.

His hand gripped hers as the elevator traveled

up. She felt the warmth of his body next to hers, just inches away, towering over her. She bit her lip, unable to look at him. She just stared at the electronic numbers displaying the floors as the elevator rose higher and higher. *Sixty-eight, sixty-nine, seventy...*

The bell dinged as the door slid open.

"After you," Darius said.

Glancing at him nervously, she stepped out directly into a dark, high-ceilinged penthouse. He followed her, as the elevator door closed silently behind them.

The rubber soles of her white shoes squeaked against the marble floor as she walked through the foyer beneath the modern crystal chandelier above. She flinched at the noise, embarrassed.

But his handsome face held no expression as he removed his long black overcoat. He didn't turn on any lights. He never looked away from her.

With a gulp, she turned away.

Gripping her purse strap, she walked forward into the shadowy main room. It was two stories high, with sparse, angular furniture in black and gray, and floor-to-ceiling windows twisted around the penthouse in every direction.

Looking from right to left, she could see the dark vista of Central Park, the high-rise buildings to the Hudson River, and the lights of New Jersey beyond it, and to the south, the skyscrapers of Midtown, including the Empire State Building, all the way to the Financial District and the gleaming One World Trade Center.

The sparkling nighttime view provided the only light in the penthouse, aside from a single blue gas fire that flickered in the stark fireplace.

"Incredible," Letty breathed, going up to the windows. Without thinking, she leaned forward, putting her overheated forehead against the cool glass, looking down at Park Avenue far below. The cars and yellow cabs looked tiny, like ants. She felt almost dizzy from being so high off the earth, up in the clouds. It was a little terrifying. "Beautiful."

His reply was husky behind her. "*You* are beautiful, Letitia."

Turning, she looked at him in the soft blue glow of firelight. Then, as she looked more closely…

Her lips parted with an intake of breath.

She'd thought Darius hadn't changed?

He'd changed completely.

At thirty-four, he was no longer a slender youth, but a powerful man. His shoulders had broadened to match his tall height, his body filling out with hard muscle. His dark hair had once been wavy and tousled, like a poet's, but was now cut short, as severe as his chiseled jawline.

Everything about Darius was tightly controlled now, from the cut of his expensive clothes—a black shirt with the top button undone, black trousers, black leather shoes—to his powerful stance. His mouth had once been expressive and tender and kind. Now his lips had a hard twist of arrogance, even cruelty.

He towered over her like a king, in his penthouse with all of New York City at his feet.

At her expression, his jaw tightened. "Letitia…"

"Letty." She managed a smile. "No one calls me Letitia anymore."

"I have never been able to forget you," he continued in a low voice. "Or that summer we were together…"

That summer. A small noise came from the back of her throat as unwanted memories filled her mind. Dancing in the meadow. Kissing the night after her debutante ball. Escaping the prying eyes of servants in Fairholme's enormous garage, steaming up the windows of her father's vintage car collection for weeks on end. She'd been ready to surrender everything.

Darius was the one who'd wanted to wait for marriage to consummate their love.

"Not until you're my wife," he'd whispered as they strained for each other, barely clothed, panting with need in the backseat of a vintage limousine. "Not until you're mine forever."

Forever never came. Their romance had been illicit, forbidden. She was barely eighteen, his boss's daughter; he was six years older, the chauffeur's son.

After a hot summer of innocent passion, her father had been infuriated when he'd discovered their romance. He'd ordered Darius off the estate. For one awful week he and Letty had been apart. Then Darius had called her.

"Let's elope," he'd said. "I'll get a day job to support us. We'll get a studio apartment in the city. Anything as long as we're together."

She'd feared it would hurt his dream of making his fortune, but she couldn't resist. They both knew there was no chance of a real wedding, not when her father would try to stop the marriage. So they'd planned to elope to Niagara Falls.

But on the night his car waited outside the Fairholme gate, Letty never showed up.

She hadn't returned any of his increasingly frantic phone calls. The next day, she'd even convinced her father to fire Eugenios Kyrillos, Darius's father, who'd been their chauffeur for twenty years.

Even then, Darius had refused to accept their breakup. He'd kept calling, until she'd sent him a single cold message.

I was only using you to get another man's attention. He's rich and can give me the life of luxury I deserve. We're engaged now. Did you really think that someone like me would ever live in a studio apartment with someone like you?

That had done the trick.

But it had been a lie. There had been no other

man. At the ripe old age of twenty-eight, Letty was still a virgin.

All these years, she'd promised herself that Darius would never know the truth. He could never know how she'd sacrificed herself, so he'd be able to follow his dreams without guilt or fear. Even if it meant he hated her.

But Darius must have finally found out the truth. It was the only explanation for him seeking her out.

"So you know why I betrayed you ten years ago?" she said in a small voice, unable to meet his eyes. "You forgive me?"

"It doesn't matter," he said roughly. "You're here now."

Her heart pounded as she saw the dark hunger in his eyes.

She looked down at the coffee stain on her uniform, the smear of ketchup near the cheerful name tag still on her left breast: LETTY! She whispered, "You can't still…want me?"

"You're wrong." He pulled her handbag off her shoulder. It felt unspeakably erotic. He pulled off her coat, dropping it to the marble floor. "I wanted you then." Cupping her face with both hands, he whispered, "I want you now."

Electricity ran up and down her body. Involuntarily, she licked her lips.

His gaze fell to her mouth.

Tangling his hands in her hair, he pulled out her ponytail, and her long dark hair tumbled down her shoulders. He stroked down her cheek, tilting back her head.

He was so much taller. He towered over her in every way.

She felt crazy butterflies, like she'd gone back in time and was eighteen again. Being with him now, all the anguish and grief and weariness of the last ten years seemed to disappear like a bad dream.

"I've missed you for so long," she choked out. "You're all I've dreamed about..."

He pressed a finger to her lips. At the contact, fire flashed from her mouth and down to her breasts. Sparks crackled between them in the shadowy penthouse, as she breathed in his woodsy, musky scent. Tension coiled low and deep in her belly.

Pulling her body tight against his own, he lowered his mouth to hers.

His kiss was hot and demanding. The stubble on his rough jawline scratched her delicate skin as he gripped her hard against him. She kissed him back with desperate need.

A low growl came from the back of his throat, and he pushed her back against the wall. His hands ran down her body to rip apart the front buttons of her white dress. She gasped as her naked skin was exposed, along with her plain white bra and panties.

"Take this off," he whispered, and he pulled her white dress off her body, dropping it to the floor.

Kneeling in front of her, he pulled off her white shoes, one by one. She was nearly naked, standing in front of the floor-to-ceiling windows that revealed the whole city.

Rising to his full height, he kissed her. His mouth plundered hers, searing her to the core. She realized her hands were unbuttoning his black shirt to feel the warmth of his skin, the hard muscles of his body. She stroked his chest, dusted with dark hair, and trembled. He felt like steel wrapped in satin, hard and soft.

She desperately wanted to feel him against her, all of him. She wanted to be lost in him—

As he kissed her, his hands roamed over her shoulders, her hips, her breasts. Her fingers twisted in his hair. She felt dizzy with longing as he pressed her against the wall, kissing her with savage desire, nipping at her lips until they bruised.

He kissed down her throat, reaching beneath the white cotton fabric of her bra to cup her bare breasts. She felt his rough warm hands against her naked skin, and her taut nipples ached, until with a low curse he reached around and unhooked the clasp of her bra.

She heard his intake of breath as it fell to the floor. She now wore only panties, while he was still fully dressed, with his black shirt unbuttoned to reveal his bare chest. As he lowered his head, taking her exposed breasts fully in his hands, her head fell back, hair tumbling down, as she gripped his bare, muscular shoulders.

She gasped as she felt the wet heat of his mouth envelop a taut nipple. Lightning shot down her body as he suckled her in his stark, shadowy penthouse, with its spectacular view of nighttime New York at their feet. She moaned softly.

Abruptly, he pulled away. She opened her eyes, feeling dizzy. Her lips parted to ask a question, but before she could remember it, he lifted her into his arms.

She didn't try to resist as he carried her through the great room into an enormous bedroom in the opposite corner. That, too, had windows on both sides, twenty feet high. She could see all of Midtown, from the Chrysler Building to the Empire State, a forest of skyscrapers between two dark rivers with their bright, moving barges.

Manhattan sparkled coldly in the dark night as Darius spread her across his bed, his expression half shadowed. He undid his cuffs and dropped his shirt to the floor.

For the first time, Letty saw the full strength of his hard-muscled torso and powerful arms. His shoulders were broad, narrowing to tight, hard abs. Removing his belt, he kicked off his shoes. Wearing just low-slung black tailored trousers, he climbed onto the bed.

Lowering his head, he kissed her against the pillows, his lips hard and rough. She felt his desire for her; she felt his heavy weight over her. Darius wanted her... He cared...

Something broke, deep inside her heart.

All this time, Letty had thought their love had ended forever. But nothing had changed, she thought in wonder, tangling her hands in his dark hair. *Nothing.* They were the same two people, still young and in love...

He slowly kissed his way down her body, his hands stroking her. She quivered, helpless beneath his touch. He dropped kisses here and there as he traversed the softness of her belly to the top edge of her white cotton panties. Drawing up, he looked down at her.

"You're mine, Letty," he whispered. "At last."

Then his heavy, hard body crushed hers deliciously, sensually. Her fingertips moved down the warm skin of his back, feeling his muscle, his spine. He moved his hips against hers, and she felt how huge and hard he was for her. Desire coiled low and deep in her belly.

He slid her white cotton panties down her thighs, down her legs. Like a whisper, they were gone.

Pushing her legs apart, he knelt at the foot of the bed. She held her breath, squeezing her eyes shut in the shadowy bedroom as he kissed the tender hollow of each foot. He moved up her calves, his fingertips caressing her skin as he lifted each knee for a slow kiss in the hollow beneath. She shivered as she felt the warmth of his breath on her thighs.

His hands moved beneath her, cupping her backside. Her thighs melted beneath his breath, hips trembling.

Finally, with agonizing slowness, he lowered his head between her legs.

Moving his hands, he kissed her inner thighs, one then the other. She felt his breath against the most intimate part of her and tried to squirm away, but he held her firmly.

Spreading her wide, he took a long, deep taste. The pleasure was intense. She choked out a gasp.

Holding her hips down against the bed, he forced her to accept the pleasure, working her with his tongue, twirling against her aching nub for long exquisite moments, then lapping her with the full width of his tongue.

She forgot to breathe, held by ruthless pleasure like a butterfly pinned to a wall. Her hips lifted involuntarily off the bed as she soared, and she gripped the white bedspread so she didn't fly up into the sky.

Waves of pleasure crashed against radiating joy. She'd never stopped loving him. And now he'd forgiven her. He wanted her. He loved her, too...

Twisting and gasping beneath his mouth, she exploded with a cry of pure happiness that seemed to last forever.

Instantly lifting his body, he pushed her arms above her head, gripping her wrists against the pillow, and positioned his hips between her legs. As she was still soaring between ecstasy and joy, he ruthlessly impaled her.

She felt him push all the way inside her, the entire enormous length of him going deep, to the heart. Her eyes flew open in shock and pain.

His back straightened at the moment he tore through the barrier that he clearly had not expected. Feeling her flinch, he looked down at her in shock.

"You were—a virgin?" he panted.

She nodded, closing her eyes and twisting her head away so he couldn't see the threatening tears. She didn't want to mar the beauty of their night, but the pain cut deep.

He held himself still inside her.

"You can't be," he said hoarsely. "How, after all these years?"

Letty looked up at him, her throat aching. And she said the only thing she could say. The words that she'd repressed for ten years, but that had never stopped burning inside her.

"Because I love you, Darius," she whispered.

CHAPTER TWO

DARIUS STARED DOWN at her. Letitia Spencer, a virgin?

Impossible. Not in a million years.

But her words shocked him even more.

"What do you mean, *you love me*?" he choked out.

Her dark eyelashes trembled against her pale skin. Then those big, beautiful hazel eyes shone up at him from the shadows of the bed as she whispered, "I never stopped loving you."

Looking down at her beautiful heart-shaped face, Darius was overwhelmed by emotion. Not the good kind, either.

He felt the cold burn of slow-rising rage.

Once, he'd loved Letty Spencer so much he'd thought he'd die without her. She'd been his angel. His goddess. He'd put her on such a pedestal, he'd even insisted they wait to make love. He'd wanted to marry her.

The memory made him writhe with shame.

How far she'd fallen. Today, she'd sent him a message—her first direct communication with him since she'd dumped him so coldly ten years before—offering him her body. For money.

All afternoon, Darius had tried to ignore her message, to laugh it off. He'd gotten over Letty years ago. He wasn't interested in paying a hundred thousand dollars to have her in his bed tonight. He didn't pay for sex. Women fought for his attention now. Supermodels fell into his bed for the price of a phone call.

But the part of him that still couldn't completely forget the past relished the idea of seeing her one last time.

Only this time, she'd be the one begging. He'd be the one to reject her.

As he'd signed the contracts that afternoon to formally sell his company, built on a mobile messaging app with five hundred million users worldwide, to a massive tech conglomerate for the price of twenty billion dollars, he'd barely listened to his lawyers droning on. Holding 90 percent of equity in the company made him the beneficiary of an eighteen-billion-dollar fortune, minus taxes.

But instead of rejoicing in the triumphant payoff of ten years of relentless work, he'd been picturing Letitia, the woman who'd once betrayed him. Imagining her trying to seduce him with an exotic dance of the seven veils. Picturing her wearing nothing but a black negligee. Begging him to take her to bed, so she could perform Olympic-level sexual feats for his pleasure.

After the papers were signed, he practically ran out of the office, away from all the congratulations and celebrations. All he could think about was Letty and her offer.

He'd spent hours trying to talk himself out of it. Then, gritting his teeth, he'd driven to the Brooklyn diner when the message said she'd be getting off work.

He didn't intend to actually sleep with her, he told himself. He'd only wanted to make her feel as small and ashamed as he'd once felt. To see her humiliated. To see her beg to give him pleasure.

Then he'd planned to tell her he no longer found her attractive, and toss the money in her face. He'd watch her take it and slink away in shame. And for the rest of his life he'd know that he'd won.

What did he care about a hundred thousand dollars? It was nothing. It would be worth it to see her abject humiliation. After her savagely calculated betrayal, he craved vengeance far more than sex.

Or so he'd thought.

But so far nothing had gone according to plan. Seeing her outside the diner, he'd been shocked at her appearance. She didn't look like a gold digger. She looked as if she were trying to be invisible, with no makeup, wearing that ridiculous white diner uniform.

But even then, he'd been drawn to her. She managed to be so damn sexy, so sweetly feminine and warm, that any man would want to help her, to take care of her. *To possess her.*

Bringing her back to the penthouse to enjoy

his vengeance, Darius had allowed himself a single kiss.

Big mistake.

As he'd felt the soft curves of her body press against his, all his plans for vengeance were forgotten against the ruthless clamor of his body. For ten years, he'd desired this woman; and now she was half-naked in his arms, willing to surrender everything.

Suddenly, it all came down to two simple facts.

She'd sold herself.

He'd bought her.

So why not take her? Why not enjoy her sensual body as a way to finally excise her memory, once and for all?

She'd lied her way through the evening, pretending it was a romantic date, instead of a commercial transaction. He'd almost been surprised.

Until now.

Naked beneath him, Letty looked up, her eyes luminous in that lovely face he'd never been able to forget.

"Say something," she said anxiously.

Darius set his jaw. After her heartless betrayal, followed by ten years of silence, she'd just told him out of the blue she loved him. What could he say in response? Go to hell?

Letitia Spencer. So beautiful. So treacherous. So poisonous.

But now, at last, he understood her goal. She

wasn't just playing for a hundred thousand dollars tonight. No. Tonight was just the sample that was supposed to leave him wanting more.

Because he'd seen her face as she left that diner. She was tired. Tired of working. Tired of being poor. Perhaps her father, newly free from prison, had been the one to suggest how to easily change her life—by becoming Darius's wife.

She must have seen his company's sale trumpeted in the newspaper today and decided it was time she made a play for his billions. He almost couldn't blame her. She'd been holding on to her virginity all these years—why not cash in?

She loved him.

Cold, sardonic anger pulsed through him.

She thought he'd learned nothing all these years. She actually thought, if she told him she loved him, he would still swoon at her feet. That he was still the lovesick idiot of long ago.

If Darius had despised her before, it was nothing compared to how he felt about her now.

And yet, he still desired her. Holding himself motionless inside her hot, tight sheath, he was still so hard, he was close to exploding.

That fact enraged him even more.

He wanted to make her pay. Not just for this last insult, but for everything that had gone before. Suddenly, causing her one night of humiliation wasn't nearly enough.

Darius wanted *vengeance*.

He wanted to raise her up, give her hope, then bring it crashing down as she'd once done. Fantastical plans coursed through his skull. He wanted to marry her, fill her with his child. He wanted to make her love him, then coldly spurn her. He wanted to take everything, and leave her penniless and alone.

That wouldn't be revenge. It would be *justice*.

"Darius?" A shadow of worry had crossed her face as she looked up at him, naked on the bed.

Lowering his head, he kissed her almost tenderly. She trembled in his arms, her plump breasts crushed against his naked chest, her amazing hips spread wide for him. Seeing her stretched out on his bed, with the play of shadows and light on the sexy curves of her tantalizing breasts, stretched the limits of his self-control.

"I'm sorry I hurt you, *agape mou*," he said in a low voice. Lie. His lips brushed the sensitive flesh of her cheek. As lightly as a butterfly setting down, he kissed the two tears that had overflowed her lashes. "But the pain won't last." Another lie. He would make sure it lasted the rest of her life. He smiled grimly. "Just wait."

She looked up at him, the picture of wide-eyed innocence. Then sighed, relaxing in surrender.

The kiss he gave her then was anything but tender. It was demanding, rough, fierce. He had experience, and she did not. He knew how to lure her. How to master her.

Unless—she could be feigning her desire?

No, he thought coldly. He would make sure she did not. That would be one insult he'd not allow her to pay. He would make sure every bit of her pleasure was real.

He stroked her soft body, taking his time, caressing her, until, slowly, she started kissing him back.

She wrapped her arms around his shoulders, pulling his weight back down on her. He shifted his hips, testing her ability to accept him, still rock hard and huge inside her. She whimpered, then exhaled, swaying her hips.

He moved expertly, drawing back slowly, then pushing inside her a second time. She gripped his shoulders, closing her eyes. He suckled a nipple, watching her face carefully. It wasn't until he saw the glow of ecstasy return to her face, and felt her muscles start to tighten around him, that he knew he'd succeeded. Triumph filled him as he began to ride her.

Filling her so deeply, this woman he'd desired for almost a third of his life, he felt light-headed. His body started to shake with pleasure so intense that it was almost like pain. They were so intertwined it was hard to know where one ended and the other began.

Pleasure and pain.

Hatred and desire.

As he thrust into her, sweat covered his body with the effort of keeping control. Her breasts swayed as he thrust inside her, all the way to the hilt. Gasping, she put her hands against the head-board, bracing against the force of his thrust. Her breathing became shallow as her body twisted beneath him with building need.

Her eyes were closed, her head tilted back, as she panted for breath. She moved her hands to his shoulders. He barely noticed her fingernails digging into his skin. He was lost in the sensation of possessing her, filling her, owning her, the glory of her flesh, the sweetness of her skin.

He felt simultaneously lost and found. Every corner of his soul that had ever felt hollow was miraculously filled. His body was pure light.

From a distance, he heard a low ragged shout and realized the sound was coming from his own mouth, releasing emotion he'd kept locked up for a decade. Her voice joined his as she cried out her own joy and grief and pain.

His body spasmed with a final, violent thrust and he poured himself into her, collapsing over her on the bed, their bodies slick with sweat, fused together.

It was much later when he opened his eyes and discovered Letty was sleeping in his arms. He stared down at her in wonder.

He wondered how he'd ever been satisfied by those pallid, skinny supermodels who had filled his bed till now. Those affairs had been insipid, hollow, dull compared to this fire. Tasting her, feeling her shake, hearing her cry of pleasure had pushed him to the limit.

It's hatred, he realized.

Hatred had made him utterly lose self-control in a way he'd never done before, in a way he'd never imagined possible. As he'd taken possession of her body, after ten years of frustrated desire, he'd slaked his ache in a dark, twisted fantasy of vengeance.

It had been the single best sexual experience of his life.

But as he pulled away from her, he sucked in his breath.

The condom had broken.

He'd worn one, of course. No matter how he might fantasize about revenge, no matter how much he hated her, the last thing he would want was to actually get her pregnant and drag an innocent child into this.

Now he stared down, unable to believe his own eyes. How could the condom have broken?

Had he been too rough, forgetting everything in his need to possess her, to relieve the savage, unrequited desire of ten years?

He'd wanted to brand her forever with the deepest mark of his possession. Had he actually wanted to fill her with his child?

A curse filled his heart.

Unraveling himself from her, he pulled away, rising naked from the bed.

He walked to the window and looked down at the bright skyscrapers of this dark city. His throat was tight as he pressed his hand against the cold glass. Catching his own reflection in the window, he was startled by the cold rage in his eyes.

Disaster. He hadn't done anything like he'd planned. He'd actually slept with Letty. And now... it might be so much worse. His hand tightened against the window. He looked back, and his jaw tightened.

Her fault, he thought. All hers.

"Are you up?" Letty murmured. "Come back to bed."

She was beneath the blankets now, looking sleepy and adorable with her dark hair tumbling over his pillows. She'd covered herself with the comforter. As if he hadn't seen everything, touched everything, tasted everything already.

His body hardened against his will, already desiring her again. He'd just had her, and he already wanted more. He wanted to take her on the bed. Against the wall. Against the window. Again and again. He stared at her in bewildered fury. Truly she was poison.

But did he really imagine after everything that had gone wrong tonight, the gold digger couldn't achieve her ultimate goal—marriage and total command, not just of his fortune, but of his body and soul?

He clawed a hand through his hair.

"Darius, what's wrong?"

He repeated flatly, "You love me?"

"It's true," she whispered.

He took a step toward the bed.

"What is it, Letty?" he said in a low voice. "Did you plan all along to renegotiate the deal? One night isn't enough, is that it? You don't want to be a rental, but a permanent sale?"

She frowned. "What are you talking about?"

Darius's jaw felt so tight it ached. Grabbing gray sweatpants from a sleek built-in drawer, he pulled them up over his naked body. He forced his shoulders to relax, forced himself to face her. When he spoke, his voice was like ice.

"You don't love me. You don't even know what the word means. When I think of how I once adored you, it sickens me. Especially now—now we both know what you really are."

Her forehead creased. "What are you talking about?"

"This night. This whole night. Don't pretend you don't know."

"I don't!"

"Don't play the outraged innocent. You sold your virginity to me for the price of a hundred thousand dollars."

For a moment, his hard words echoed in the shadowy bedroom. The two of them stared at each other in silence.

"What are you talking about?"

"Your email," he said impatiently. "Claiming you needed to pay off some mobster who'd broken your father's arm and threatened to break his whole body if he didn't come up with a hundred thousand dollars within the week." He tilted his head curiously. "Is it true? Or just a convenient excuse?"

Her eyes were wide. "My father's broken arm…" She seemed to shudder as she pulled the blankets up higher against her neck. "I never sent any message."

His lips curved sardonically. "So who did?"

Letty's cheeks were bright red. "I…" Running her hand over her eyes, she said, "So that's why you came for me? You were buying a night in bed?"

"What did you think?"

"I thought…" She faltered. "I thought you'd forgiven me for what I did…"

He snorted. "Ten years ago? You did me a favor. I've been better off without you. Your other fiancé must have realized that fast, since he didn't bother to stick around, either." His jaw set. "What I'll never forgive is what you and your father did to my dad. He died an early death because of you. Lost his job, his life savings. He lost everything, had a heart attack and died." He bared his teeth in a sharklike smile. "Because of you."

"Darius, it's not what you think," she blurted out. "I…"

"Oh, is this the part where you come up with an explanation that makes you look like an innocent saint?" he drawled. "Go on, Letty. Tell me how your betrayal was actually a favor. Explain how you destroyed my family at great personal sacrifice, because you loved me so much." His voice dripped contempt. "Tell me all about your *love*."

She opened her mouth.

Then snapped it closed.

Darius's lip twisted coldly. "That's what I thought."

She blinked fast, her beautiful eyes anguished. She took a deep breath and spoke one small word. "Please…"

But mercy had been burned from his soul. He shrugged. "I thought it would be amusing to see you again. I didn't actually intend to sleep with you, but you were so willing, I finally thought, why not?" He sighed as if bored. "But though I paid for the whole night, I find I've already lost interest." Leaning forward, he confided, "And just as one entrepreneur to another, you sold yourself too cheaply. You could have bartered for a higher price with your virginity. Just a suggestion as you go forward with your new career. What is it called now? Paid mistress? Professional girlfriend?"

"How can you be so cruel?" She shook her head. "When you came to the diner tonight, I saw the same boy I loved…"

"Really?" He tilted his head, quirking a dark eyebrow. "Oh. Right. Since you'd kept your virginity in reserve all these years, you thought if you tossed in a little romance, I'd fall for you like a stone, just like I did back then. 'I love you, Darius. I never stopped loving you,'" he mimicked mockingly.

"Stop!" she cried, covering her ears with her hands. "Please stop!"

Some of her blanket had slipped where she sat on his bed, revealing a curvy breast. He could see the faint pink tip of her nipple, and he could still taste the sweetness of her, still remember how it had felt to be deep inside her.

His breath came hard. Sleeping with her hadn't satiated his desire. To the contrary. He only wanted her more.

The fact she still had such power over him was infuriating.

Turning sharply, he went to his desk. He pulled a cashier's check from a leather binder. Returning to the bed, he tossed it toward her.

"There. I believe this concludes our business."

Letty's lovely face looked dazed as she picked up the cashier's check from the bed. She looked at it.

"If you have another client tonight, don't let me keep you," he drawled.

She briefly closed her eyes and whispered, "You're a monster."

"*I'm* a monster." He barked a low, cruel laugh. "Me?"

Turning away, she rose naked from the bed. He waited, wondering for a split second if she'd toss the check in his face and prove him wrong. If she did...

But she didn't. She just picked up her panties from the floor and walked to the door. He sneered at himself for being naive enough to even imagine the possibility she'd give up her hard-earned money for the sake of honor, or even pride!

She left the bedroom, going out into the great room of the penthouse. He followed, watching as she collected her bra and shoes, then scooped her white dress from the floor. Putting it on after slipping on her panties, she buttoned the dress quickly, leaving gaps where he'd ripped off buttons in his haste to get it off her. She wouldn't meet his eyes.

Darius wanted to force her to look at him. He wanted her humiliated. He wanted her heartbroken. His pride demanded something he couldn't name. *More.*

She stuffed her bra in her handbag and put her bare feet into her shoes and turned to go.

"It's just a shame the condom broke," he said.

She froze. "What?"

"The condom. Of course I was wearing one. But it broke. So if you wind up pregnant, let me know, won't you?" He gave a hard smile. "We will negotiate a good price."

He was rewarded. She finally turned and looked at him, aghast.

"You'd pay me? For a baby?"

He said coldly, "Why not, when I paid you for

the act that created it?" His expression hardened. "I will never marry you, Letty. So your attempt at gold digging ends with that check in your bag. If by some unfortunate chance you become pregnant, selling me our baby would be your only option."

"You're crazy!"

"And you disgust me." He came closer to her, his eyes cold. "I would never allow any child of mine to be raised by you and that criminal you call a father. I would hire a hundred lawyers first," he said softly, "and drive you both into the sea."

For a moment, Letty looked at him, wide-eyed. Then she turned away with a stumble, but not before he saw the sheen of tears in her eyes. She'd become quite the little actress, he thought.

"Please take me home," she whispered.

"Take you home?" Darius gave a sardonic laugh. "You're an employee, not a guest. A temporary employee whose time is now done." His lip curled. "Find your own way home."

CHAPTER THREE

LETTY SHIVERED IN the darkest, coldest hours of the night as she walked to the Lexington Avenue subway station and got on the express train. It was past one in the morning, and she held her bag tightly in the mostly empty compartment, feeling vulnerable and alone.

Arriving at her stop in Brooklyn, she came numbly down the stairs from the elevated station and walked the blocks to her apartment. The streets were dark, the shops all closed. The February—no, it was March now; it was past midnight—wind was icy against her cheeks still raw with tears.

She'd thought it was a miracle when she saw Darius again. She'd thought he'd found out the truth of how she'd sacrificed herself, and he'd come back for her.

Telling him she loved him had felt so right. She'd honestly thought he might tell her the same thing.

How could she have been so wrong?

You disgust me.

She could still hear the contempt in his voice. Wiping her eyes hard, she shivered, trembling as she trudged toward her four-story apartment building.

While many of the nearby buildings were nice, well kept, with flower boxes, hers was an eyesore, with a rickety fire escape clinging to a crumbling brick facade. But the place was cheap, and the landlord had asked no personal questions, which was what she cared about. Plugging in a security code, Letty pushed open the door.

Inside, the temperature felt colder. Two of the foyer's lights were burned out, leaving only a single bare lightbulb to illuminate the mailboxes and the old delivery menus littering the corners of the cracked tile floor.

Even in the middle of the night, noises echoed against the concrete stairwell, a Doppler tangle of tenants yelling, dogs barking, a baby crying. A sour smell came up from beneath the metal stairs as she wearily climbed three flights. She felt wretched, body and soul, torn between her body's sweet ache from their lovemaking and her heart's incandescent grief.

The fourth floor had worn, stained carpet and a bare lightbulb hanging from the ceiling. Going past the doors of her neighbors—some of whom she'd never met even after three years—she reached into her handbag, found her keys and unlocked the dead bolt. The door creaked as she pushed it open.

"Letty! You're back!" Her father looked up eagerly from his easy chair. He'd waited up for her, wrapped in both a robe and a blanket over his flannel pajamas, since the thermostat didn't work properly. Turning off the television, he looked up hopefully. "Well?"

As the door swung shut behind her, Letty stared at him in disbelief. Her handbag dropped to the floor.

"How could you?" she choked out.

"How could I get you and Darius back together so easily?" Her father beamed at her. "All I needed was a good excuse!"

Her voice caught on a sob. "Are you kidding?"

Howard frowned. "Are you and Darius not back together?"

"Of course we're not! How could you send him a message, pretending to be me? Offering me for the night!"

"I was trying to help," he said falteringly. "You've loved him for so long but refused to contact him. Or he you. I thought…"

"What? That if you forced us together, we'd immediately fall back into each other's arms?"

"Well, yes."

As she stared at him, still trembling from the roller coaster of emotion of that night, anger rushed through her.

"You didn't do it for me!" Reaching into her bag, she grabbed the cashier's check and shoved it at him. "You did it for this!"

Her father's hands shook as he grasped the cashier's check. Seeing the amount, his eyes filled with visible relief. "Thank God."

"How could you?" She wanted to shake her father and scream at him for what he'd done. "How could you sell me?"

"*Sell* you?" Her father looked up incredulously. "I didn't sell you!" Struggling to untangle himself from his blanket, he rose from his chair and sat beside her on the sofa. "I figured the two of you would talk and soon realize how you'd been set up. I thought you'd both have a good laugh, and it would be easier for you each to get over your pride. Maybe he'd send money, maybe he wouldn't." His voice cracked. "But either way, you'd be together again. The two of you love each other."

"You did it for love." Letty's eyes narrowed skeptically. "So the fact that you read about Darius's billion-dollar deal this morning had nothing to do with it."

He winced at her sarcasm, then looked down at the floor. His voice trembled a little as he said, "I guess I thought there was no harm in also trying to solve a problem of my own with a…dissatisfied customer."

Glaring at him, Letty opened her mouth to say the cruel words he deserved to hear. Words she'd never be able to take back. Words neither one of them would ever be able to forget. Words that would take her anguish and rage, wrap them up into a tight ball and launch them at her father like a grenade.

Then she looked at him, old and forlorn, sitting

beside her on the sagging sofa. The man she'd once admired and still absolutely loved.

His hair had become white and wispy, barely covering his spotted scalp. His face, once so hearty and handsome, was gaunt with deep wrinkles on his cheeks. He'd shrunk, become thin and bowed. His robe was too big on him now. His near decade in prison had aged him thirty years.

Howard Spencer, a middle-class kid from Oklahoma, had come to New York and built a fortune with only his charm and a good head for numbers. He'd fallen in love with Constance Langford, the only daughter of an old aristocratic family on Long Island. The Langfords had little money left beyond the Fairholme estate, which was in hock up to the eyeballs. But Howard Spencer, delirious with happiness at their marriage, had assured Constance she'd never worry about money again.

He'd kept his promise. While his wife had been alive, he'd been careful and smart and lucky with his investment fund. It was only after his wife's sudden death that he'd become reckless, taking bigger and bigger financial risks, until his once respected hedge fund became a hollowed-out Ponzi scheme, and suddenly eight billion dollars were gone.

The months of Howard's arrest and trial had been awful for Letty, and worrying about him in prison had been even worse. But now, as she looked at the old man he'd somehow become, was the worst of all.

As she looked at his slumped shoulders, his heartbroken eyes—at his broken arm, still hanging uselessly in the cast—she felt her anger evaporate, leaving in its place only grief and despair. Her mouth snapped shut.

Slumping forward, she covered her face with her hands.

The memory of Darius's words floated back to her. *You needed to pay off some mobster who'd broken your father's arm and threatened to break his whole body if he didn't come up with a hundred thousand dollars within the week.*

Chilled, she looked up. "Why didn't you tell me someone broke your arm, Dad? Why did you let me think it was an accident?"

Howard looked down at the floor guiltily. "I didn't want you to worry."

"Worry?" she cried.

His wan cheeks turned pink. "A father's supposed to take care of his daughter, not the other way around."

"So it's true? Some thug broke your arm and threatened you if you didn't pay him back his money?"

"I knew I could handle it." He tried to smile. "And I have. Once I sign over this check, everything will be fine."

"How do you know you won't have more thugs

demanding money, once it's known you actually paid someone back?"

Her father looked shocked. "No. Most of the people who invested in my fund were good, civilized people. Not violent!"

Letty ground her teeth. For a man who'd been in a minimum-security federal prison for nine years, he could be surprisingly naive.

"You should have told me."

"Why? What would you have done except worry? Or worse—try to talk to the man yourself and put yourself in danger?" He set his jaw. "Like I said, I didn't know if Darius would actually send the money. But I knew, either way, you would be safe because you'd be with him." He shook his head, trying to smile. "I really thought you and Darius would take one look at each other and be happy again."

Letty sagged back against the sofa cushions. Her father'd really thought he was doing her a favor. That he was reuniting her with a lost love. That he was protecting her, saving her.

She whispered bleakly, "Darius thought I was a gold digger."

Howard looked indignant. "Of course he didn't! Once you told him you hadn't sent the message…"

"He didn't believe me."

"Then…then…he must have believed you were just a good daughter looking out for your father. Darius has so much money now, you can't tell me he'll miss such a small amount. Not after everything you did for *him*!"

"Stop," she choked out. Just remembering how Darius had looked at her when he handed her the cashier's check was enough to make her want to die. But after he'd told her about the threat against her father's life, what choice had she had?

Her father looked bewildered. "Didn't you tell him what happened ten years ago? Why you never ran away with him?"

She flinched as she remembered Darius's acid words. *Go on, Letty. Tell me how your betrayal was actually a favor. Explain how you destroyed my family at great personal sacrifice, because you loved me so much.*

"No," she whispered, "and I never will. Darius doesn't love me. He hates me more than ever."

Howard's wrinkled face looked mournful. "Oh, sweetheart."

"But now I hate him, too." She looked up. "That's the one good thing that happened tonight. *Now I hate him, too.*"

Her father looked anguished. "That was never what I wanted!"

"It's good." Wiping her eyes, she tried to smile. "I've wasted too many years dreaming of him. Missing him. I'm done."

She was.

The Darius Kyrillos she'd loved no longer existed. She saw that now. She'd tried to give him everything, and he'd seduced her with a cold heart. Her love for Darius was burned out of her forever. Her only hope was to try to forget.

But four weeks later, she found out how impossible that would be. She'd never be able to forget Darius Kyrillos now.

She was pregnant with his baby.

She'd taken the pregnancy test, sure it would be negative. When it was positive, she was shocked. But shock soon became a happy daze as Letty imagined a sweet fat baby in her arms, to cuddle and adore.

Then she told her father.

"I'm going to be a grandfather?" Howard was enraptured at the news. "That's wonderful! And when you tell Darius—"

That caused the first chill of fear. Because Letty suddenly recalled this baby wouldn't just be hers, but Darius's.

He hated her.

He'd threatened to take her baby from her.

Letty shook her head violently. "I can never tell him about the baby!"

"Of course you will." Her father patted her on the shoulder. "I know you're angry at him. He must have hurt you very badly. But that's all in the past! A man has a right to know he's going to be a father."

"Why?" She turned to him numbly. "So he can

try to take the baby away because he hates me so much?"

"Take the baby?" Her father laughed. "Once Darius finds out you're pregnant, he'll forget his anger and remember how much he loves you. You'll see. The baby will bring you together."

She shook her head. "You're living in a dream world. He told me…"

"What?"

Letty turned away, hearing the echo of that coldly malevolent voice. *I would never allow any child of mine to be raised by you and that criminal you call a father.*

"We need to start saving money," she whispered. "Now."

"Why? Once you're married, money will never be a worry for you again." Howard looked ecstatic. "You and my grandchild will always be cared for."

Letty knew her father couldn't believe Darius wanted to hurt her. But she knew he did.

I would hire a hundred lawyers first and drive you both into the sea.

They had to leave this city as soon as possible.

Under the terms of her father's probation, Howard was required to remain in the state of New York. So they'd go north, move to some little town upstate where no one knew them, where she could find a new job.

There was just one problem. Moving required money. First and last month's rent, a security deposit and transport for Letty, Howard and all their belongings. Money they didn't have. They were barely keeping their heads above water as it was.

Over the next few months, Letty's fears were proved true. No matter how hard she worked, she couldn't save money. Howard was always hungry or needed something urgently. Money disappeared. There were also the added expenses of medical co-payments for Letty's doctor visits, and physical therapy for her father's arm.

There was some good fortune. After Howard had paid off the mobster, no other angry former investors had threatened him, demanding repayment.

But there, their luck ended. Just when Letty was desperate for overtime pay, all the other waitstaff suddenly seemed to want it, too. But warmer summer weather meant fewer customers at the diner craving the fried eggs and chicken fried steak that were the diner's specialties. Her work hours became less, not more.

Each morning when she left for work, her father pretended to look through job listings in the paper, looking shifty-eyed and pale. Pregnancy exhausted her. Each night when she got home from work, almost falling asleep where she stood, she cooked dinner for them both. She'd do the dishes and go to bed. Then the whole day would start again.

Every day, she anxiously counted the savings she kept in her old chipped cookie jar on the kitchen counter. And every day, she looked at the calendar and felt more afraid.

By late August, amid the sticky heat of New York City, Letty was growing frantic. She could no longer hide her baby bump, not even with her father's oversize shirts. Everyone at the diner knew she was pregnant, including her friend and co-worker Belle Langtry, who kept teasing her about it.

"Who's the father?" Belle demanded. "Is it Prince Charming? I swear I saw you leave here once with a dark-haired man in a sports car."

No. It wasn't Prince Charming, Letty thought numbly. Her baby's father was no prince, but a selfish, coldhearted beast who wanted to steal her child away.

Finally, as her yearlong lease on the apartment ended, she knew she couldn't wait any longer. She gave two weeks' notice at the diner. She still hadn't saved enough money, but time had run out.

On the first of September, Letty splashed cold water on her face in the darkness before dawn, then looked at her drawn face in the mirror.

Today was the day.

They couldn't rent a truck to move their belongings. No money for that. Instead, they'd just take what would fit in two suitcases on the bus.

They'd have to leave behind all the final memories from Fairholme. From her childhood. From her mother.

The thought made her throat ache.

But Letty was six months pregnant now. Her heart pounded as she put her hand protectively over her baby bump. She knew from the ultrasound at the doctor's office that she was expecting a boy. How had time fled so quickly? In less than three months, by late November, she'd be cuddling her sweet baby in her arms.

Or else she'd be weeping as the baby's cold-hearted father took him away from her forever. She still remembered Darius's cold, dark eyes, heard the flat echo of his voice.

If by some unfortunate chance you become pregnant, selling me our baby would be your only option.

She was suddenly terrified she'd waited too long to leave New York.

Going into the tiny kitchen, she tried to keep her voice cheerful as she said, "Dad, I'm going to pick up my last paycheck, then buy bus tickets."

"I still don't understand why Rochester," he said with a scowl.

She sighed. "I told you. My friend Belle knows someone who knows someone who might be able to get me a job there. Everyone says it's nice. I need you to start packing."

"I have other plans today." His voice was peevish.

"Dad, our lease is up in two days. I know it's not fun, but whatever you don't pack, I'm going to have to call the junk dealer to take." Her throat ached. Maybe all their leftover stuff *was* junk, but it was all they had left. Of Fairholme. Of her mother. Her voice tightened. "Look, I know it won't be easy."

Sitting at the peeling Formica table where he was doing the crossword, Howard glared at her with irritation. "You just need to tell that man of yours you're pregnant."

They'd been having this argument for months. She gritted her teeth. "I can't. I told you."

"Poppycock. A man should be given the opportunity to take care of his own child. And you know, Letty," he added gruffly, "I won't always be here to look after you."

Howard—look after her? When was the last time that had been true, instead of the other way around? She looked at her father, then sighed. "Why don't you believe me?"

"I knew Darius as a boy." Fiddling with his untouched coffee mug, he looked at her seriously. "If you'd just help him see past his anger, he's got a good heart—"

"I'm not gambling on his *good heart*," she said bitterly. "Not after the way he treated me."

Her father looked thoughtful. "I could just call him..."

"No!" Letty shouted. Her eyes blazed. "If you ever go behind my back like that again, I will never talk to you for the rest of my life. Do you understand? *Never.*"

"Okay, okay," he grumbled. "But he's your baby's father. You should just marry him and be happy."

That left her speechless for a minute.

"Just be packed by the time I return," she said finally, and she went out into the gray, rainy September morning. She picked up her last check at the diner—for a pitiful amount, but every dollar would help—and said farewell to her fellow waitress Belle, who'd moved to New York from Texas the previous Christmas.

"Anytime you need anything, you call me, you hear?" Belle hugged her fiercely. "No matter where you are, Rochester or Rome, remember I'm only a phone call away!"

Letty didn't make friends easily, so it was hard to say goodbye to the only real friend she'd made since she'd left Fairholme. The thought of going to yet another new apartment in a new town where she didn't know anyone, in hopes of starting a job that might not even exist, filled her with dread. She tried to smile.

"You too, Belle," she managed. Then, wiping her eyes, she said goodbye to everyone else at the diner and went back out into the rain to deposit her check at the bank and get two one-way bus tickets to Rochester.

When Letty got back home, her hair and clothes were damp with rain. Her father wasn't at the apartment, and his suitcases were empty. All their belongings were still untouched, exactly where she'd left them.

She'd just sort through everything herself, she thought wearily. Once she'd figured out how many boxes they'd have to leave behind, she'd call the junk dealer.

Of the eight billion dollars her father's investment fund had lost, three billion had since been recovered. But the authorities had been careful not to leave him with anything of value. Their possessions had been picked over long ago by the Feds and bankruptcy court.

What was left was all crammed into this tiny apartment. The broken flute her mother had played at Juilliard. The ceramic animals Constance had painted for her daughter as gifts, starting with her first birthday. The leather-bound classic books from her grandfather's collection, water-damaged, so worthless. Except to them. Her great-grandfather's old ship in a bottle. Her grandma Spencer's homemade Christmas ornaments. All would have to be left.

We'll get through it, Letty told herself fiercely. They could still be happy. She'd raise her baby with love, in a snug cottage overlooking a garden of flowers. Her son would have a happy childhood, just as Letty had.

He wouldn't be raised in some stark gray penthouse without a mother, without love...

Letty started digging through the first pile of

clutter. She planned to stay up the whole night scrubbing down the apartment, in hopes their landlord might actually give back her security deposit.

Hearing a hard knock at the door, she rose to her feet, overwhelmed with relief. Her father had come back to help. He must have forgotten his key again. Sorting through their possessions would be so much easier with two of them—

Opening the door, she gasped.

Darius stood in her doorway, dressed in a black button-down shirt with well-cut jeans that showed the rugged lines of his powerful body. It was barely noon, but his jaw was dark with five-o'clock shadow.

For a moment, even hating and fearing him as she did, Letty was dazzled by that ruthless masculine beauty.

"Letty," he greeted her coldly. Then his eyes dropped to her baby bump.

With an intake of breath, Letty tried to shut the door in his face.

He blocked her with his powerful shoulder and pushed his way into her apartment.

been not only justified, but righteous. The boys in school had never taunted him again.

But this time, his grandmother had been proved right, because...

CHAPTER FOUR

SIX MONTHS AGO Darius had wanted vengeance.

He'd gotten it. He'd ruthlessly taken Letitia Spencer's virginity, then tossed her out into a cold winter's night. He'd seduced her, insulted her. He'd thrown the money in her face, made her feel cheap.

It had been delicious.

But since then, to his dismay, he'd discovered the price of that vengeance.

In Darius's childhood, back on the Greek island where he was born, his grandmother had often told him that vengeance hurt the person who committed it worse than the one who endured it. When the kids at school mocked his illegitimate birth, sneering at his mother's abandonment—*Even your own mitéra didn't want you*—his grandmother had told him to ignore them, to take the high road.

He'd tried, but the boys' taunts had only grown worse until he was finally forced to punch them. They'd all been bloodied in the fight, but especially Darius, since it had been one against four.

"So you see I'm right," his grandmother had said gravely, bandaging him afterward. "You were hurt worse."

In Darius's own opinion, that vengeance had

been not only justified, but strategic. The boys at school had never taunted him again.

But this time, his grandmother had been proved right. Because Darius's vengeance against Letty had hurt him more than he'd ever imagined.

Instead of quenching the flame, that night together had only built his desire for her into a blazing fire.

He wanted her. Every night for the last six months, he'd half expected Letty to contact him. Once her prideful anger had faded, surely she would want him back—if not for his body, then obviously for his money.

But she never had. And when he'd remembered the haunted look on her beautiful heart-shaped face the night she'd told him she loved him, the night he'd taken her virginity and tossed her ruthlessly into the dark, he'd had moments when he'd wondered if he might have been wrong.

But how could he be wrong? The evidence spoke for itself.

Still, in the months since their night together, his continual raw desire for her had made him edgy. He'd intended to remain as his company's CEO for a year, guiding his team in the transition after the sale. Instead, he'd gotten into an argument with the head of the conglomerate and left within weeks. Darius could no longer endure working for someone else, but he'd signed a noncompete clause, so couldn't start a new business in the same field.

Bereft of the twenty-hour workdays that had been the entirety of his life for a decade, he hadn't known how to fill his hours. He tried spending some of his fortune. He'd bought a race car, then ten cars, then a race track. He'd bought four planes, all with interiors done in different colors. No. Next he'd tried extreme sports: skydiving, heli-skiing. Yawn.

Worst of all, he'd been surrounded by beautiful women, all keen to get his attention. And he hadn't wanted a single one of them.

He'd been *bored*. Worse. He'd felt frustrated and angry. Because even with the endless freedom of time and money, he couldn't have what he really wanted.

Letty.

Now, seeing her in the flesh, so beautiful—so *pregnant*—he hated himself for ever taking his vengeance. No matter how richly she'd deserved it, look where that thrill of hatred and lust had led.

Pregnant. With his baby.

Even wearing an oversize white T-shirt and baggy jeans, Letty was somehow more sensual, more delectable, than any stick-thin model in a skintight cocktail dress. Letty's pregnancy curves were lush. Her skin glowed. Her breasts had grown enormous. With effort, he forced his gaze down to her belly.

"So it's true," he said in a low voice. "You're pregnant."

She looked frozen. Then she squared her shoulders, tossing her dark ponytail in a futile gesture of bravado. "So?"

"Is the baby mine?"

"Yours?" Her eyes shot sparks of fire, even though she had dark shadows beneath, as if she hadn't been sleeping well. "What makes you think the baby's yours? Maybe I slept with ten men since our night. Maybe I slept with a hundred—"

The thought of her sleeping with other men made Darius sick. "You're lying."

"How do you know?"

"Because your father told me."

The fight went out of her. She went pale. "My... my father?"

"He wanted me to pay for the information, but when I refused, he told me everything. For free."

"Maybe he was lying," she said weakly. She looked as if she might faint.

"Sit down," Darius ordered. "I'll get you a glass of water. Then we'll talk."

She sank into the old pullout sofa, her cheeks pale. It wasn't hard for him to find the kitchen. The apartment was pathetically small—just a postage-stamp-sized living room, surrounded by an even smaller bedroom, bathroom and kitchen.

He looked around him, amazed that the onetime heiress of Fairholme, born into a forty-room mansion, was now living with her father in an apartment the same size as the room her mother had once used to arrange flowers off the solarium.

Old boxes and mementos were packed everywhere. The leftovers of her family's former life—items that obviously weren't valuable enough to be sold, but too precious to be thrown away—were clustered around the old television and piled tightly along the walls. A pillow and folded blanket sat beside the pullout sofa.

Darius walked across the worn carpet to the peeling linoleum of the telephone-booth-sized kitchen. Dust motes floated in the weak gray sunlight. The barred window overlooked an air shaft that faced other apartments, just a few feet away. With the bars across the window, it felt like prison.

It's better than they deserve, he told himself firmly. And it was still nicer than his childhood home in Heraklios. At least this place had electricity, running water. At least this place had a parent.

Darius's own parents had both left him, in different ways, two days after he was born. His unemployed father had discovered his newborn son crying in a basket by his door, left out in the rain by his former lover, a wealthy, spoiled heiress who'd abandoned the child she'd never wanted.

Fired from his job, Eugenios Kyrillos found himself unable to get another. No other rich Greek fathers, it seemed, wanted to risk their daughters' virtue to a chauffeur who didn't know his place. Desperate to find work, he'd departed for America, leaving his baby son to be raised by his grandmother in the desolate house by the sea.

The first time Darius had spoken to his father in person had been at his grandmother's funeral, when he was eleven. Then his father had taken him from Greece, away from everything and everyone he'd ever known, and brought him to America.

Fairholme had seemed like an exotic palace, where everyone spoke a language he couldn't understand. His father had seemed just as strange, the emotionally distant chauffeur of this grand American king—Howard Spencer.

And look what the Spencers had come to now.

Darius had long ago torn down his grandmother's shack in Heraklios and built a palatial villa. He had a penthouse in Manhattan, a ski chalet in Switzerland, his private race track outside London. His personal fortune was greater than anything Howard Spencer ever dreamed of.

And the Spencers were now living in this tiny, threadbare apartment.

But instead of feeling a sense of triumph, Darius felt strangely unsettled as he walked through her dreary kitchen and poured a glass of water from the tap. Returning to the equally depressing living room, he handed Letty the glass, then looked at the folded blankets and pillow on the floor.

"Who sleeps on the sofa?"

Letty's cheeks turned pink as she looked down at the sagging cushions. "I do."

"You pay all the rent, and your father gets the bedroom?"

"He hasn't been sleeping well. I just want him to be comfortable."

Darius looked at her incredulously. "And you're pregnant."

"What do you care?" she said bitterly. "You're just here to take my baby away."

Well. True. His eyes fell on the empty suitcases. "Where were you planning to go?"

"Anywhere you couldn't find us."

Darius stared down at her grimly. After his conversation with Howard Spencer, he'd had his investigator check up on Letty and found she'd only recently left her job as a waitress. She was still broke. None of the other employees remembered seeing any men around her, except one waitress, Belle, who had described Darius himself.

It seemed that, contrary to all previous assumptions, Letty wasn't a gold digger. Not with other men.

Not even with Darius.

In that, he'd misjudged her. After the way Letty had crushed him so devastatingly ten years ago, informing him that she was leaving him for a richer man, he'd believed Letty was a fortune hunter to the core.

It made sense. His own mother had abandoned him as a two-day-old newborn for the exact same reason. To Calla, Darius had been the embarrassing result of a one-night liaison with her wealthy family's chauffeur. She'd been determined to marry as befitted her station. She'd cared only about money and the social position that went with it.

But Letty wasn't the same. At least not anymore.

Darius abruptly sat down on the sofa beside her. "Why didn't you come to me when you found out you were pregnant? You had to know I would give you everything you needed and more."

"Give? I knew you'd only take!" she said incredulously. "You threatened me!"

He ground his teeth. "We could have come to some arrangement."

"You threatened to buy my baby, and if I tried to refuse, you would take the baby from me and—what were your words?—drive me into the sea?"

Darius didn't like to be reminded of what he'd said six months ago. He'd rationalized his cruelty on the grounds of justice. But now…strictly speaking, he might have sounded a little less than civil, if not outright crazy. Irritated, he glared at her. "Drink your water."

"Why? What did you put into it?" She sniffed the glass. "Some drug to make me pass out so you can kidnap me to a Park Avenue dungeon?"

He snorted a laugh in spite of himself. "The water came from your tap. Drink it or not. I just thought you looked pale."

She stared at him for a moment, then took a tentative sip.

He looked around the tiny apartment. "Why are you living here?"

"Sadly, the presidential suite at the St. Regis was already booked."

"I mean it, Letty. Why did you stay in New York all these years? You could have just left. Moved west where no one would know you or care about what your father did."

She blinked fast. "I couldn't abandon him. I love him."

The man was a liar and a cheat, so of course Letty loved him. And she'd intended to raise their baby with him in the house, the man Darius blamed for his own father's death. He ground his teeth. "Are you even taking care of yourself? Do you have a doctor?"

"Of course," she said, stung. "How can you ask me that?"

"Because you've been working on your feet all day, until recently. And living in a place like this." He gestured angrily around the threadbare, cluttered apartment. "It never occurred to you I'd want better for our child?"

She glared at him. "*I* wanted better! I wanted my baby's father to be a good man I could trust and love. Instead, I got you, Darius, the worst man on earth!"

"You didn't think so ten years ago."

He immediately wished he could take the words

back, because they insinuated that he still cared. Which he didn't.

"Oh, you're actually willing to talk about ten years ago? Fine. Let's talk about it." She briefly closed her eyes. "The reason I never showed up the night we were supposed to elope was because I was protecting you."

His lip curled scornfully. *"Protecting* me."

"Yes." Her expression was cool. "The day we were going to elope, my father told me his investment fund was a fraud. It had stopped making money years before, but he'd continued making payouts to old investors by taking money from new ones. The Feds were already on his tail. I knew what was going to happen." She lifted her luminous gaze. "I couldn't let you get dragged into it. Not with all your big dreams. You'd just started your tech company..." She took a deep breath and whispered, "I couldn't let my father's crime ruin your life, too."

For a moment, Darius's heart twisted as he looked at her beautiful face, her heartbreaking hazel eyes. Then he remembered that he no longer had any heart vulnerable enough to break.

"You're lying. You left me for another man. A rich man who could—how did you express it?— *give you the life of luxury you deserved.*" He snorted. "Though obviously he wasn't much good. He must have dumped you the moment your father was arrested."

"He couldn't dump me." She gave a low laugh. "He never existed."

"What?"

"It was the only way I knew you'd let me go." She lifted her chin and added with deliberate lightness, "I knew your weakness, even then."

"Weakness?" he growled.

"You always said a man could be measured by his money. I knew you wouldn't accept my just breaking up with you without explanation. So I gave you one. I told you I wanted someone richer. I knew you'd believe that."

He stared at her. "It's not true."

"I've always been a terrible liar." She looked sad. "But you still believed it. And immediately stopped calling me."

Darius's cheeks burned as he remembered how he'd felt that day. She was right.

He had loved her beyond reason, had been determined to fight for her at any cost. Until she'd told him she didn't want him because he was poor. He'd believed it instantly. Because money made the man. No money, no man.

His throat felt tight as he looked at her, struggling not to believe she was telling the truth when every fiber of him believed her.

"And my father?" he said hoarsely. "Were you protecting him, too—getting him fired?"

"It's true. I did have him fired. I told Dad I couldn't bear to look at Eugenios because he reminded me of you. I did it because I was afraid my dad might ask him to invest his life savings in the bankrupt investment fund. My dad still believed he could fix everything then. I knew your father would give him his savings. He was loyal to the core."

"Yes, he was," he bit out. His father had always made his employer his top priority, even over his own son.

Darius couldn't remember when his father had ever put his son first, over his job. He hadn't attended Darius's school events, not even his high school graduation. Being eternally at Howard Spencer's beck and call, keeping the ten luxury cars all gleaming and ready, had been Eugenios's total focus in life.

Oh, his father had fed and clothed him and given him a place to live in the two-bedroom apartment over the Fairholme garage that went with his job. But emotionally, they were oceans apart. The two men never talked.

Until that one awful day Darius told his father what he really thought of him…

But that memory was so white-hot with pain, he pushed it from his mind with all the force of a ball thrown from the earth to the moon.

Letty sighed beside him on the sofa. "I was trying to get your father away from Fairholme before he lost everything. But it was too late. He'd already invested his life savings years before. My dad had accepted it for his fund, even though it was such a small amount," she said in a small voice. "As a favor."

A small amount? His father's life savings! The arrogance of them! Darius's dark eyebrows lowered in fury.

"Howard Spencer is a liar and cheat," he said harshly. "He destroyed people's lives."

"I know," she whispered, looking down. She bit her full, rosy lower lip. "He never meant to."

"He deserves to suffer."

She looked up. "He has suffered. During his arrest and trial, I tried so hard to be strong for him. When he was in prison, I was there every visiting day. I cheered him up. Encouraged him. And all the time, I felt so scared. So alone." She gave him a watery smile. "Sometimes the only thing I had to cling to was you."

"Me?"

"At least I hadn't dragged you down with me," she whispered. "At least you were able to follow your dreams."

Darius stared at her in shock.

Then he narrowed his eyes. She was trying to take credit for his accomplishments. To claim that if not for her sacrifice, he never would have made his fortune. She thought so little of him. Ice chilled his heart.

"And you expect me to be grateful?"

She looked startled. "I—"

"When you found out about your father's crime," he said tightly, "you should have come to me. I was your future husband. Instead, you lied to me. You cut me out of your life. Rather than asking for my help, you apparently believed I was so incompetent and useless, you felt you had to sacrifice yourself to save me."

"No," she gasped, "you've got it all wrong…"

"You never respected me." He forced his voice to remain calm when his shoulders were tight with repressed fury. "Not my intelligence, my judgment or my strength."

"Respected you?" she choked out. "*I loved you.* But I knew what was about to happen. I couldn't let you drown with us. You had nothing—"

"You're right," he said coldly. "I had nothing. No money. No influence. You knew I couldn't pay for lawyers or speak to politicians on your behalf. So you decided I was useless."

"No." She looked pale. "I just meant you had nothing to do with it—"

"You were my fiancée. I had *everything* to do with it. I would have tried to protect you, to comfort you. But you never gave me the chance. Because you believed I would fail."

Her voice sounded strangled. "Darius—"

He held up his hand sharply. "But now I have made my fortune. Everything has changed. And yet you still intended to disappear and keep my child secret from me for the rest of your life." A new, chilling thought occurred to him. "What story did you intend to tell the baby, Letty?"

"I don't know," she whispered.

"What were you going to raise my child to believe? That he or she had no father? That I hadn't wanted him?" An old childhood grief he'd thought long buried suddenly shook the ground beneath his feet, like an earthquake threatening to swallow him whole. "That I'd purposefully abandoned him?"

"I don't know!" Letty cried. "But you said you'd take the baby from me. I had no choice but to run!"

Darius stared at the woman he'd known for most of his life. He'd loved her for such a short, sweet time. He'd hated her far longer.

He himself had been abandoned by everyone who should have loved him as a child. His whole young life he'd never felt like he really belonged anywhere.

And then there was Letty.

He'd loved her so wildly, so truly, so recklessly. She had finally destroyed what was left of his heart. That had been Darius's final lesson.

He was determined that his child would never learn such a lesson.

Darius's jaw tightened. His child would be surrounded by love from the beginning. His son or daughter would have a solid place in the world and never doubt their worth.

The blindfold of rage and hurt pride lifted from his eyes. He looked at Letty, and suddenly everything became crystal clear. Calm settled over him like rain.

Their child needed both of them.

For the last decade, he'd tried to forget about the Letty he'd once known. About her character. About her kind heart.

He saw now that in Letty's mind, her hurtful lies a decade before hadn't shown disrespect, but love. She really had been trying to protect him. As she still was trying to protect her father.

As she was trying now, in her own misguided way, to protect their child.

Letty hadn't betrayed him. She'd loved him, as recently as February, the night they'd conceived their child. Yes, she'd shown bad judgment ten years ago, lying to him, hiding the truth about her father. She'd continued to show bad judgment today, planning to run away with his child. A chill went down his spine to think of what might have happened if her father hadn't called him today.

But it wasn't entirely her fault. Her love blinded her. It made her weak. And after the cold way he'd treated her, and his threats to take the child, he couldn't blame her for being afraid.

It didn't make her a monster. It wasn't enough of a reason to brutally separate her from their child. Not after he himself had known what it was to have no mother. No father. No real place in the world.

Their baby would have both parents and a secure, settled home.

Darius knew he had to rebuild Letty's trust in him. He had to find a way to strengthen her occasionally faulty judgment with his own. If Darius was wiser, it was because he never allowed love to blind him. He always focused on the bottom line. So what was it here?

The answer was simple.

He had to make Letty his wife.

It was the only way to properly secure their child's future. It would guarantee the stability of two parents and a permanent home.

And also, his body suddenly whispered, marrying Letty would permanently secure her in his bed.

The thought electrified him. That settled it.

"I misjudged you," he said.

Letty glared at him. "Yes!"

"I treated you badly."

"You think?"

"So let me make up for it now." Leaning toward her on the sofa, Darius said, "I want you to marry me, Letty."

Her jaw dropped. "Marry you!"

"I've realized now I blamed everything on you. It wasn't your fault…"

"No."

"It was your father's," he finished grimly. "He's ruined your life. I won't let him ruin our child's."

Her eyes were wide as she put her hands over her large belly. "You're crazy. My father loves the baby, just as he loves me!"

"And what about the next time some thug decides to attack him? What if that man decides to hurt your father's family instead?"

Letty's expression became troubled. Swallowing, she whispered, "That wouldn't happen…"

"No. It won't. Because you and the baby will be miles away from Howard Spencer and safe with me." He rose abruptly to his feet. "You will have to sign a prenuptial agreement…"

"I won't, because I'm not going to marry you."

She wasn't joking or playing coy. She actually sounded serious.

Darius stared down at her in confusion. So many women were dying to marry him, he'd assumed that Letty—jobless, penniless, faced with threats on all sides—would be thrilled at the thought of being his bride. "Of course you want to marry me."

"Marry someone I hate? Who hates me back? No, thanks."

He couldn't believe she was trying to fight him when it was the only practical solution. He gritted his teeth. It was that idea of *love*, once again interfering with all common sense!

"Have you thought this through?" Folding his arms, he regarded her coolly. "I could take you to court. Have you declared an unfit mother, selfishly placing our child at risk."

Letty rose to her feet in turn, matching him toe-to-toe, though he was bigger by a foot in height and at least sixty pounds of muscle. She narrowed her eyes. "You could *try*."

In spite of himself, he almost smiled. Another thing he'd forgotten about her character. She fought harder for others than she ever did for herself.

"You really think you can handle a custody battle? You think there are waves of lawyers out there, willing to support Howard Spencer's daughter pro bono, when all they'd get for their trouble is a lot of bad PR?"

Her cheeks flushed, even as she lifted her chin defiantly. "We'll see, won't we?"

But beneath her bravado, her expression was soft and sad. Her long dark ponytail gleamed in waves down her back, and his eyes strayed to the roundness of her belly and full breasts, voluptuous beyond belief. In this moment, Darius thought she looked like everything desirable in a woman—the perfect image of what any man would dream of in a wife.

He suddenly imagined how she might look in court. Whatever her father's sins, if she did find a good attorney, she could be packaged and sold to the presiding judge as the poor, innocent, poverty-stricken waitress threatened by the cold, power-hungry billionaire. No matter how many legal sharks he hired, Darius wasn't guaranteed to win. There was some small possibility he might lose.

He abruptly changed tack.

"Does our baby deserve to have parents at war?

Living in here—" he motioned to the peeling wallpaper, the cracked ceiling "—instead of my penthouse? Does he deserve to grow up in poverty without the protection of his father's name? Without my love?"

Letty looked stricken. "Our baby could still have your love."

"He deserves everything I can provide. Are you really so selfish as to make our child suffer for the sake of your own angry pride?"

He saw emotions struggle on her face. She really was a terrible liar. He knew he was very close to getting what he wanted—her total surrender.

"We could make our marriage work," he murmured. "Our son or daughter would be our priority, always."

"Son," she said unwillingly.

He looked at her sharply.

She took a deep breath, then slowly smiled. "We're having a boy."

"A boy!" The nebulous idea of a baby suddenly solidified in Darius's mind. He could imagine his son smiling, playing soccer, laughing, hugging him. And the fact that she'd revealed that detail proved how close she was to agreeing to his proposal. His resolve solidified. Stepping closer, he said softly, "Marry me, Letty."

Looking uncertain, she bit her lip. "It would be a disaster. Not just for me. For you. Don't you know how much people hate me?"

"Not once you're with me," he said confidently.

"You don't understand how bad it is…"

"I'm sure you're exaggerating." He'd all but won. Now that his unborn child was secure, he was already jumping ahead to the thought of enjoying Letty's surrender in full, imagining her naked and writhing with desire in his arms. He wanted to take her back to the penthouse immediately. Then he remembered. "I am hosting a charity event tonight. The Fall Ball."

She looked impressed in spite of herself. "You're hosting that this year?"

"We can announce our engagement to all of New York."

"It's a mistake!"

"Let me worry about that."

"Okay, but…"

"But what?"

A shadow crossed her face. "But I don't love you anymore."

He felt a strange emotion, deep down inside. He crushed it down before he could identify what it was.

"I do not need your love. I can assure you that you'll never have mine. Love is for children. I just need your compliance." When she still hesitated, he took a deliberate step back. "Or I can walk out that door and go straight to my lawyer."

Letty looked wistful in the gray light from

the small window. She sighed sadly. "Have it your way."

"You'll marry me?"

She nodded.

He felt a surge of smug masculine triumph. "Good choice."

Pulling her roughly into his arms, he did what he'd yearned to do for six months and kissed her.

From the moment he felt her lips against his and tasted her sweetness—her mouth, her tongue— he was lost, and at the same time, found. Her lips parted, and as she melted against him, he savored her surrender. His body and long-dead soul roared back to life.

Letty wrenched away. "But first, you'll take me to your charity ball tonight. And see firsthand what it would be like to actually have me as your wife."

"Good—"

"Just remember." She gave him a crooked smile. "You asked for it."

CHAPTER FIVE

LETTY ALMOST DIDN'T leave a note for her father. Her anger at his betrayal was too high. But in the end she didn't want him to worry, so she scribbled a note and left it on the counter.

Out with Darius, and I'm never talking to you again.

Darius had taken one look at her closet and told her he was taking her shopping for the ball. She'd tried to protest, but he'd retorted, "There's no point in announcing our engagement if you turn up at the ball dressed in rags. No one would believe it."

"Fine," she said sulkily. "Waste your money on a ball gown. See if I care."

But she had the sudden disconcerting feeling that her life was no longer her own.

As she climbed into his sports car, her stomach growled with hunger. But she vowed she wasn't going to say a word about it. It was bad enough he was buying her a dress. She wasn't going to ask him for food, like a beggar!

But as Darius climbed into the driver's seat beside her, all her senses went on high alert. Having him so close did strange things to her insides. As he drove through the busy traffic, she glanced at him out of the corner of her eye. His dark hair wasn't even mussed, and his powerful body was relaxed in the leather seat. He looked so much calmer than she felt.

But why wouldn't he be relaxed?

He'd won.

She'd lost.

Simple as that.

Or so Darius thought. Letty clasped her hands together in her lap as she looked out the window. Once he actually saw what life would be like for him with her at his side, he wouldn't be able to get rid of her fast enough. Maybe she and her father could still be on that bus to Rochester tomorrow.

Darius didn't yet see that her family's scandal wasn't something he could master or control. That was why he'd been so angry that she'd protected him ten years ago with her silence. He still somehow thought, if he'd known the truth back then, he could have prevented disaster.

She looked up through the window, seeing flashes of blue sky between the skyscrapers like a strobe light. Darius would get a dose of reality today. He'd discover how toxic the Spencer name was, even now. It had been even worse at the time of her father's arrest and trial, when reporters and angry, tomato-throwing hecklers had camped outside her father's pied-à-terre on Central Park West!

Let Darius get just a glimpse of what he would have been up against if she'd actually followed her heart and married him ten years ago instead of setting him free. He didn't appreciate the way she'd tried to protect him? Fine. Still staring out the window, she wiped her eyes hard. Let him just see.

The rain had stopped. The sky was blue and bright on the first of September. As they drove through Manhattan, puddle-dotted sidewalks were full of gawking tourists, standing still like islands as a current of New Yorkers rushed past them, coming up from the subway, hurrying back to work after lunch.

When their car stopped at a red light, Letty glanced at a fancy chauffeured town car stopped beside them. In the backseat, she saw a man speaking angrily into his phone and staring at a computer tablet, totally wrapped in his own bubble. Rich people lived in a separate world. Letty hadn't fully realized that.

Not until she'd fallen out of it.

After her father's confession that awful night long ago, after she'd tried her best to protect Darius and his father by getting them away from the manor, she'd begged Howard to go to the police and throw himself on their mercy.

He'd loved her, so a few months later he'd done it.

The police and Feds had descended on him like

the hard-case criminal they believed him to be. Within six months, he was in prison on a nine-year sentence.

Letty had tried to remain in one of the exclusive small towns on Long Island near Fairholme. But it proved impossible. Too many people recognized her and didn't hesitate to yell or even—more than once—physically take the few dollars in her wallet, saying her father owed them. Manhattan had been even worse, and anyway was way out of her price range. So she'd moved to a working-class neighborhood in Brooklyn where she could be anonymous. No one bothered her. Mostly, people were kind.

But without money or family or friends, Letty had learned the hard way what it meant to struggle and always have too much month at the end of her paycheck.

No one likes self-pity. Help someone else, baby. Letty could almost hear the whisper of her mother's voice, so kind, so warm, so loving. Almost see her mother's eyes glowing with love. *The best way to feel better when you're sad is to help someone who's hurting more.*

Good advice.

Taking a deep breath, Letty turned to Darius in the sports car. "So tell me about your charity, the one benefiting from the Fall Ball tonight."

Driving, he glanced at her out of the corner of his eye. "It provides college scholarships for foster kids."

"Nice," she said, surprised. "But I never pegged you as the society-ball-hosting type."

He shrugged. "I have the time. Might as well use it."

"You could just waste your days dating beautiful women and spending your obscene amounts of money."

He pulled his car to a curb where a valet waited. "That's exactly what I plan to do today."

"You're going on a date?" Then she saw his look and realized he meant her. She blushed. "Oh."

The door opened, and Letty stepped out onto Fifth Avenue, which was lined with exclusive designer shops from famous international brands to quirky boutiques less well-known but every bit as expensive. The last time she'd shopped on this street she'd been a pampered seventeen-year-old looking for a white dress for the graduation ceremony at her private school, Miss Parker's. She hadn't fit into society, even then. She'd been too bookish, too tenderhearted, too socially awkward.

But now Letty was actually scared. She glanced at the people coming out of an exclusive department store, almost expecting one of them to tell her to get lost, that she no longer belonged here.

"Which shop first?" Darius asked, his dark eyes smiling.

"I changed my mind," she muttered. "I don't want to go."

The smile disappeared. "Too late for that."

"Darius…"

Ignoring her protests, he grabbed her hand. Letty tried not to notice the sizzle of electricity from their touching palms as he pulled her into a famous luxury store.

As soon as they passed the doorman into the store's foyer, a salesgirl came up to them, offering a tray of champagne. "Monsieur?"

He took a glass. "Thank you."

Noting Letty's pregnant belly, the salesgirl didn't offer champagne. "And for madame? Some sparkling water, perhaps, some juice of *pamplemousse*?"

"No, thanks," Letty said, pulling away from Darius. Ducking her head, she pretended to look through the nearest dress racks, sparsely and expensively filled with garments that seemed to be designed for a size zero.

"We require assistance," he said.

"Sir?"

He turned to an elegant white-haired woman, apparently the manager, dressed in an expensive-looking tweed suit. "I need a ball gown for my fiancée."

Fiancée. The word made Letty shiver. But it was true, in a way. She'd agreed to his marriage proposal.

It's not a real engagement, she told herself firmly. She glanced down at her bare left hand. There was no ring. No ring meant it wasn't real.

Anyway, the engagement would be over before the end of the night.

"Couture or ready-to-wear, Mr. Kyrillos?" The white-haired woman somehow already knew who he was.

"It's for tonight."

"We can, of course, do any last-minute alterations that madame may require. If you'll please come this way?"

They were led to a private area with a white leather sofa and a three-way mirror, as a succession of salesgirls, under the sharp-eyed direction of the manager, brought in clothes.

"She'll try on everything," Darius said, standing in front of the sofa as his cell phone rang. Lifting it from his pocket, he told Letty, "Come out when you have something to show me."

As salesgirls filled her arms with gowns and gently pushed her toward the changing room, she hesitated. "What do you want to see?"

Looking her body over slowly, Darius gave her a heavy-lidded sensual smile. "Everything."

Beneath his hot gaze, somehow, he made her feel like a goddess of sex—even at six months pregnant, in her old T-shirt and jeans!

Darius sat down calmly on the white leather sofa, talking into his phone and sipping champagne. She turned away with a sigh to try on gowns for a ball that she was dreading.

Maybe it wouldn't be all bad, she tried to tell

herself. She couldn't remember the last time she'd had new clothes. Everything in her closet was either from high school or purchased from the bargain bin at the thrift store. It might be fun to get a dress that was not only pretty, but actually fit.

Then she saw the price tag of the first gown.

Darius looked up expectantly when she came out of the dressing room. His expression changed to a scowl. "Why are you still in your old clothes?"

"The price of these gowns is ridiculous! We can go to the local thrift shop and find a barely used prom dress…"

"Letty."

"I mean it. It's foolish for you to throw money away when you might never see me again after tonight."

"Now you're talking nonsense." He tilted his head, looking her over critically. "Are you not feeling well? Are you hungry? Thirsty? Tired?"

She wasn't going to say a word about being hungry. Wild horses couldn't drag it out of her!

Her stomach growled again.

"Um. I might have missed breakfast."

It wasn't her fault! The baby made her say it!

He looked mad. "You should have told me." He grabbed a glass of sparkling mineral water from a salesgirl. "Here," he said gravely, pushing it into her hand. "Start with that. Breakfast or lunch?"

The cool water tasted delicious, and did make her feel slightly better. "Breakfast?"

Turning to one of the hovering assistants, he ordered, "Have a large breakfast sent down from your café."

"Oh, sir." The salesgirl looked sorrowful. "I'm afraid that's impossible…"

"Of course it's possible for Mr. Kyrillos," the white-haired manager snapped, turning to them with a bright smile. "A pregnant woman must never go hungry. What would madame like?"

"Everything," Darius said. "Send down a tray or two. We'll be here a while. We need a ball gown, but also a great deal more. Shoes, accessories, maternity clothes. Price is no object. We may be here for hours."

"Yes, sir," the woman replied happily, clapping her hands at her assistants, who rushed to obey.

"Darius, you don't need to make a fuss!"

"You're wrong. I can see all too well that I need to be in charge. Because you've always been better at taking care of others than yourself." He drew Letty gently to the white sofa. "Here. Sit down. Take a breath."

"But I left all those dresses in the changing room—"

"They will wait. Relax. You do not have to shop hungry. Breakfast is on its way."

The white leather cushion shifted beneath them, tipping her toward him on the sofa. The edge of her thigh brushed against his. She jumped away with an intake of breath, looking up at him with big eyes.

"I'm not your responsibility."

"You are now." Reaching out, he tucked a long tendril of her dark hair back behind her ear and said softly, "And taking care of you will be my pleasure."

His...pleasure?

A sudden terrifying thought occurred to her.

"Darius," she said haltingly, unable to meet his eyes. "You surely can't think…"

"Think what?"

Taking her courage in her hands, she looked into his dark wicked eyes. However charming he might seem at the moment, she couldn't forget the heartless man he'd revealed himself to be. She couldn't let herself confuse him with the boy she'd once loved. No matter how much Darius's dark eyes, his smile, his kindness might seem the same. *He was nothing like the man she'd loved.*

"You can't think…" She took a deep breath. "That our marriage would be real."

"Of course it will be real. Legal in any court."

"I mean…" She licked her lips, hating him for making her spell it out. "It would just be a marriage of convenience, nothing more. For our baby. We wouldn't… You and I, we would never…"

"You will sleep in my bed, Letty." His dark eyes burned through her. "Naked. Every single night."

His sensual voice swirled around her body like a hot wind, making her toes curl.

She had to resist. She had no intention of sleeping with him again, no matter how seductive he might be. She'd been a virgin till twenty-eight, waiting for love. That love was gone.

"I loved you the night we conceived our baby. Everything has changed. Unlike you, I can't have sex with a cold heart," she said in a low voice. "No love, no sex."

He wrapped her hand in his larger one. She felt his palm against hers, and a shiver ricocheted through Letty's body, deep, to blood and bone. He leaned forward.

"We'll see," he whispered.

CHAPTER SIX

LETTY WAS SAVED when the salesgirls interrupted them with trays of pastries and fruit and juices, followed closely behind by yet more racks of clothes for her to consider.

A proper breakfast tray soon followed with maple bacon pancakes drizzled in maple syrup, hash brown potatoes and hot fried sausages. Thus fortified, Letty spent another hour trying on all the clothes she liked in that luxury store. Then they moved to a designer boutique. Then an exclusive department store.

By the end of the afternoon, Darius had bought her so many bags of clothes, he'd had to call his bodyguard and driver down to Fifth Avenue to carry everything back to the penthouse.

He took her to a world-famous jewelry store where they were ushered to an exclusive, private floor. She tried to protest, for about the thirtieth time. "You really don't need to keep spending more money on me!"

Darius held up a twenty-carat diamond necklace with a critical eye. "You're going to be my wife. Of course you need clothes."

"Those are diamonds."

He grinned. "Hard, sparkling clothes."

She harrumphed. "You're wasting your money."

"So let me waste it. What do you care?" Lifting his eyebrow, he said mildly, "I seem to recall your saying you hate me. So why not make me suffer?"

Why not indeed? Put that way, it didn't sound so unreasonable. "You do have it coming."

Setting the necklace down, he looked at her with a heavily lidded gaze.

"And I intend to take it." Turning back to the jeweler, he nodded toward the diamond necklace. "Starting with that."

But though Darius insisted on buying her an entire wardrobe of fancy clothes, he was never satisfied by any of the ball gowns she tried on. Truth be told, even Letty thought most of them hideous. A hoop skirt on a baby bump? She looked like a cartoon hippo.

In spite of Letty's misgivings, the afternoon flew by in an irresistible whirlwind of small pleasures. Her new wardrobe wasn't comprised of minimalist black and gray clothes as he had originally suggested, currently popular with chic society women, nor were they the plain, sensible, washing-machine-ready clothes she'd worn for the last ten years. No.

Darius had watched her carefully as she'd tried on each outfit, and he seemed to notice the colors that made her face light up with joy. Bright, vivid jewel tones—emerald green, cerulean blue, fuchsia, ruby red—in impractical sensual fabrics like silk.

"We'll take it," he would say immediately.

Letty felt guilty revealing her own pleasure, but she couldn't help herself. For so long, survival had been her only goal. She couldn't remember the last time that her happiness had mattered to anyone, least of all her.

But Darius treated her as if her happiness was actually the main goal.

Because I carry his baby inside me, she told herself, as she changed her clothes yet again in a private dressing room.

But his hot dark gaze had told her it was more than that. He didn't just want custody over their baby.

He wanted to possess Letty, too.

You will sleep in my bed. Naked. Every single night.

She shivered, then tried on yet another formal gown, this one made of a slinky knit fabric in a delicious shade of hot pink, her favorite color.

The dress fell softly over her body. Reaching back, she couldn't quite zip it all the way. She looked at herself in the mirror.

The long stretchy gown fit perfectly over her pregnant body, curving over her full breasts and huge belly. She liked it, but weren't pregnant women supposed to wear tent dresses?

"I want to see," Darius's voice commanded outside the dressing room. She took a deep breath, then came out, her cheeks hot.

"What do you think?" she said timidly.

His expression said everything. He walked slowly around her, looking up and down her body in a way that made her shiver inside.

"That," he said softly, "is the dress."

She bit her lip. "I'm afraid it's too formfitting…"

"It's perfect."

"I couldn't zip it all the way up…"

Drawing close, he wrapped his arms around her. She felt his arms brush against her body as he pulled on the zipper. His eyes never left hers as he towered over her, so close. He made her breathless.

A hint of a smile lifted the edges of his cruel, sensual mouth. He cupped her cheek, then stroked down her throat. "The necklace will be perfect here. Against your skin."

Looking down, she realized how low cut the gown was. Her cheeks went redder. "I shouldn't wear this."

"Why?"

"It's too revealing. Everyone will stare."

"They will stare regardless."

"Because I'm the daughter of a criminal."

"Because you're an incredibly beautiful woman."

At his soft words, Letty's throat suddenly hurt. "You don't realize how much they hate me." Her eyes stung as she pushed away. "When they see me…it'll be like dropping raw meat in a shark tank. And the more they notice me, the more they'll rip me apart." She took a deep breath, tried to smile. "I sound like I'm complaining. I'm not. I can handle it. I'm used to it. But…"

"But what?"

She looked down at the floor.

"Letty?"

She said in a small voice, "I don't want them to say rude things about you at your own party. And they will if I'm your date."

Reaching out, he lifted her chin. "I can take care of myself, *agape mou*," he said in a low voice. "When will you learn that?"

His dark gaze fell to her mouth, and Letty's whole body tightened as, for a moment, she wondered if he was going to kiss her, right there in the luxurious store. For a wild moment, it didn't seem like such a bad idea.

He turned to the nearest salesgirl. "We'll take this dress. Wrap it up. We need shoes to match."

Letty tried on ten pairs before she found stiletto heels that made her gasp at their outrageous beauty.

"Those," Darius said, looking at Letty's face.

"No, I couldn't possibly. They're too impractical. I'll never wear them again!" She looked doubtfully at her feet, wobbling in the high heels. "I'm not even sure I can wear them now."

But even as she protested, she couldn't look

away from the beautiful shoes, which were en-crusted with glittery pink crystals and had a red sole.

"We'll take them," he told the salesgirl firmly.

Though they pinched Letty's toes and made her wobble ever so slightly, she was filled with joy as she sat down and handed the precious pink crys-tal stilettos to the salesgirl. She couldn't remem-ber the last time she'd had anything so outrageous, just because of their beauty. And their cost! She was trying not to think about owning shoes worth three months' rent. And when would she ever wear them again? Working as a waitress? Going to the grocery store?

It was wicked, letting him buy her these shoes. Letting him buy her so many things, when after tonight, he'd likely never want to see her again.

She would just leave everything behind, she de-cided. Most of the clothes could be returned, un-worn, with tags. She'd have nothing to feel guilty about when he tossed her out of his life. Nothing!

"Now—" Darius's gaze lingered on her lips, then dropped lower "—lingerie."

Letty made a sound like a squeak. "Forget it!"

"Ah. You intend to wear nothing beneath your gown tonight? I approve."

Her cheeks burned. "Of course I'm going to wear something!"

"Then you need undergarments." He nodded toward three hovering salesgirls. "Get us a selection of lingerie that would suit the gown."

They departed in a rush to obey.

"I hope you don't expect me to try *those* on for you," Letty said sulkily.

"No?" He looked at her lazily. "Maybe later."

Her blush deepened.

Right here, in the exclusive department store, with strangers everywhere, Darius was looking at Letty as if he wanted nothing more than to drag her into a changing room and roughly make love to her. Possibly while she was wearing nothing but those pink crystal stilettos. Not a bad idea...

She blinked, realizing she'd been licking her lips. She put her hand unsteadily to her head. What was happening? Was she losing all her morals over a pair of beautiful shoes and for the body of a dangerously beautiful man?

Except Darius wasn't just beautiful. He was also the only man she'd ever slept with. The only man she'd ever been in love with. She was even now carrying his child deep inside her. He wanted her in his bed. He wanted to marry her. All of those things together were likely to distract any woman.

And with every moment, she felt herself being drawn into his world. Remembering what it was like when money was no object. To be without worry or care.

To be cherished.

It had been a long time since she'd felt that way.

She'd been a lonely teenager, far happier spending her time with the estate staff, pets or books instead of other debutantes. At fourteen, she'd fallen hopelessly for Darius, the chauffeur's son, six years older and totally out of her league. Funny now to recall that she'd actually imagined herself to be unhappy then.

She'd discovered soon after what unhappiness really meant, when her beloved mother, the heart of their home, had suddenly fallen ill. She'd wasted away and died within months.

Her father had been gutted. A few years later, he'd gone to prison. Letty had tried to be tough. She'd tried to be strong. She'd hadn't let herself think. Hadn't let herself feel.

But now...

For the first time in years she realized how it felt to be truly looked after. To be cared for. As the salesgirls wrapped up a thousand dollars' worth of silky lingerie, she tried to tell herself it was just an illusion. Exactly like Cinderella. After midnight tonight it would all disappear.

Darius signed the credit card receipt, smiling at her out of the corner of his eye. "Is there anything else you desire?"

Letty looked at him, her heart in her throat. Then she just shook her head.

"It's growing late." He took her hand. "We have one more place to go."

The bodyguard had already left in Darius's

sports car filled with bags. As his driver walked ahead, weighed down by yet more bags, toward the waiting town car, Darius never let go of her hand. His dark eyes glowed down at her as the sun slipped down between the skyscrapers, toward a horizon she couldn't see.

Maybe it was the pregnancy hormones, but as they climbed into the back of the elegant car, emotion squeezed her heart as she looked at him. All day, Darius had been beside her, ready to push through any crowds, to make sure that she got— in his opinion—proper attention. When she was thirsty, when she was hungry, when she was tired, he seemed to know even before she did, and like a miracle, whatever she desired would instantly appear.

It was as if she were no longer alone. Someone else was looking out for her. Someone tough and strong. Someone who made her feel safe.

Safe?

She shook herself hard. Darius was dangerous. Selfish. Arrogant and cold.

He frowned at her in the backseat. "Are you crying?"

She wiped her tears. "Nope."

"Letty."

"I'm sorry. I just…" She faltered. "You've been so kind."

"Buying you clothes?" he said incredulously. He gave a low laugh. "Is that all it takes?"

It was more than the clothes, far more, but she couldn't explain. She said miserably, "I shouldn't go with you to the ball tonight."

His mouth turned down grimly. "You're going."

"Don't you understand? It'll only cause you trouble."

"Stop trying to protect me," he said evenly. "I mean it."

"But—"

"It's not your job to protect me. It's my job to protect you now. And our baby. Never again insult me by insinuating I am incapable of it." At her expression, he said more gently, "Don't you understand, Letty? I will watch over you. I'll make sure no one ever hurts you again. You'll always be taken care of now. You're safe."

She was suddenly shaking as the town car drove down the street. How she wished it were true! How she wished she could believe in him, as she had so long ago.

The car door opened. Looking up in surprise at Darius's driver, who was holding it open, Letty looked back at Darius. He gave her a cheeky grin.

"I'm just dropping you off. This is the best day spa in the city. Collins is bringing your gown and everything else you'll need for the ball tonight. I'll collect you here at eight."

"A day spa? Why?"

"You deserve some pampering. Enjoy yourself." He leaned forward in the car's backseat. She felt his warmth and breathed in his scent as he brushed back her hair and whispered in her ear, "I'll be back for you soon."

As he drew back, her heart beat rapidly, and she felt prickles of sensation and desire course through her body, down her spine and over her skin.

And all he'd done was whisper in her ear!

Oh, this was bad.

Her legs were shaky as she stepped out of the car and was whisked into the gorgeously bright day spa with its tall windows, green plants and kitschy pink furniture. A team of specialists, including massage therapists, beauty therapists, stylists and more, surrounded her, moaning about Letty's cuticles, her tense shoulders, her dry skin…

Hours passed in a flash. Her nails were done and her muscles rubbed and her skin freshened until dewy. Hairstylists and makeup artists came next, and once they were done, it was nearly eight.

Letty put on the new silk bra and panties, the perfectly fitting pink gown and sparkly stiletto heels. She looked at herself in the mirror.

Her long, freshly shaped dark hair was now glossy and shiny and bouncy from the hairstylist's efforts. Red lipstick made her look glamorous, and her eyes were emphasized with dark liner and even a few false eyelashes for drama. Her full breasts, pushed up by the bra, were laid out like a platter in the knit pink dress, her hips thrust forward by the stilettos, her voluptuous belly the star.

She was dazzled by her own image. She barely recognized herself.

"Wait until Mr. Kyrillos sees you," the proprietress of the spa said with a broad smile. "Our finest creation!" There was a whisper, then a gasp. "He's here!"

Nervously, Letty came down into the foyer. She wondered if he would think she looked silly. She couldn't bear it if her appearance embarrassed him, on top of everything else.

But as Darius came into the foyer, she saw his face. And she knew he approved. Deeply.

"You look incredible," he whispered. "So beautiful."

She gave him a shy smile. "You don't look so bad yourself."

The truth was, she couldn't take her eyes off him. His hard jaw was freshly shaved, and his dark eyes wickedly bright. He looked impossibly handsome, tall and broad-shouldered in his sophisticated black tuxedo, which was obviously tailored. No tuxedo off the rack could have fit his muscled body so perfectly.

Wordlessly, Darius held out his arm.

Wrapping her hand around his hard, thick bicep, she shivered, remembering how six months ago, she'd felt his naked, powerful body over hers. Inside hers. She nearly stumbled at the memory.

He stopped.

"Sorry, I'm still getting the hang of my shoes,"

she lied. She couldn't explain that it wasn't the stilettos that had made her stumble, but the memory of that hot February night they'd conceived their baby.

A night that would never happen again, she thought wistfully. After tonight, he'd run away from her so fast that there would be flames left on the ground, like in a cartoon.

This time, a limousine waited for them. Collins, the driver, wore his formal uniform with a peaked cap as he held open her passenger door.

"Where is the ball this year?" she asked Darius.

"The Corlandt," he said, naming a venue that was nearly as famous as the Met or Frick or Whitney.

She gulped. It was even worse than she'd thought. As the limo took them uptown, she felt sick with dread. She looked out the window, frantically trying to build ice around her heart and get herself back into a place where she was too well armored to feel any attack.

But her newly scrubbed skin felt far too thin now. Wearing this beautiful dress, and being with Darius, she felt vulnerable. She felt visible. She felt raw.

Even though she no longer loved him, she still didn't want him hurt because of her. She tried to tell herself it would be for his own good, so he'd realize they had no future. But she couldn't bear the thought of what was about to happen.

All too soon, the limo arrived. Looking out at the crowds and red carpet and paparazzi, Letty couldn't breathe. Collins got out and opened their door.

Darius went first. There was a low roar from the crowds, watching from behind the cordons of the red carpet, at seeing Darius Kyrillos, the host of the evening and currently New York's most famous billionaire bachelor, get out of the limo, gorgeous in his tuxedo. As cameras flashed in the darkening twilight, he gave a brusque wave.

Looking at the photographers, Letty felt so weak she wasn't sure she could get out of the limo.

Turning back, Darius held out his hand to where she sat quivering in the backseat. He lifted a challenging eyebrow.

Shaking, Letty put her hand in his.

As she exited the limo, a low murmur started amid the photographers and press waiting outside the red carpet as someone recognized Letty.

Then it spread.

There was a gasp of recognition traveling among the photographers and crowd like a rumble of thunder rolling across the ground. The camera flashes went crazy as journalists and celebrity bloggers started screaming at her.

"Letitia Spencer!"

"Where have you been for the last ten years?"

"How does it feel now that your father's out of prison?"

"Do you feel guilty for your father's victims as you're coming to a ball in diamonds?"

"Are you two together?"

"Mr. Kyrillos, with all the city at your feet, why would you date a jailbird's daughter?"

Darius responded only with a glower as he arrogantly walked past them, Letty gripping his hand tightly. He led her past the reporters and inside the magnificent beaux-arts-style granite building. Only after she'd walked up the steps and past the imposing columns through the oversize door, and he'd shut it behind them, did she exhale. Immediately, he pulled her close. Letty closed her eyes, still shaking as she breathed in his strength, his warmth, his comfort.

"It's over," he said softly as he finally drew back, tucking back a dark tendril of her hair behind her ear. "That wasn't so bad, was it?"

"You think it's over?" She gave him a trembling smile. "It's only just begun."

Darius's expression darkened, but they were interrupted as a famous white-haired society matron covered in jewels entered the foyer behind them. Her face brightened when she saw Darius. She immediately left her much younger date to come forward and give him air-kisses.

"Darius, how lovely to see you! Thank you again for hosting this important event." She simpered. "Though I think there will be many broken hearts when they see you brought a date—"

But as the matron turned to Letty, her smile froze. Her expression changed to shock, then outrage.

"Hello, Mrs. Alexander," Letty said bashfully. "I don't know if you remember, but I used to go to school with your daughter, Poppy. We were both debutantes at the—"

"Stop." The woman's eyes blazed. "Don't you dare speak to me." Looking back at Darius, she hissed, "Do you know who this girl is? What she's done?"

He looked at her coldly. "Of course I know who Letty is. We've been friends since childhood. And as for what she's done—I think you have her confused with her father."

The woman turned to Letty with narrowed eyes. "You have some nerve coming here. Your father stole money from nearly every person attending tonight." She looked at Darius incredulously. "And you are insane to bring her. Take my advice. Send Letitia Spencer straight out the door. Or you might find that you suddenly have no guests, and your charity will suffer. For what? So you can get that little tart in your bed?" She looked pointedly at Letty's belly. "Or perhaps you did that already?"

Letty's cheeks went hot. She suddenly felt like a tart, too, wearing this low-cut, formfitting pink dress that showed off every curve. Beneath the society matron's scrutiny, even her beautiful sparkly shoes lost their gleam, and suddenly just pinched her feet.

"It's only out of respect for those poor foster children that I'm not leaving here right now." The woman glared between them, then flounced away in her jewels and fluttering silk sleeves.

Letty was left paralyzed from the ambush.

"Don't listen to her," Darius said, putting his hand on her shoulder. "She's a witch."

"I don't blame her for being mad," Letty said in a low voice. "Her family lost a lot of money. Tens of millions."

"It obviously hasn't cut into her jewelry and plastic-surgery budget. Forget her. Let's go in."

Wrapping her arm securely over his, he marched her into the ballroom as cheerfully as a revolutionary leading a French aristocrat to the guillotine.

But it was no good. The rest of the evening was just as Letty had feared. As lovely and magical as the afternoon had been, the ball sucked the joy out of everything.

Darius insisted on keeping her by his side as he greeted his society guests, each of whom had paid thousands of dollars to attend this ball, ostensibly for the benefit of college scholarships for foster kids but mostly just to have a good excuse to party with friends and show off new couture.

Letty felt their hostile stares, though with Darius beside her, none were as brave or foolhardy as Mrs. Alexander. None of them said anything to her face. Instead, the cream of New York society just stared at her in bewildered horror, as if she had a contagious and fatal disease, then looked at Darius as if they were waiting for him to reveal the punch line of whatever joke had inspired him to bring a pariah like Letitia Spencer to the Fall Ball when he could have had any beauty in the city for the asking.

She heard whispers and felt their hard stares as she and Darius passed through the crowds in the ballroom. When he briefly left her to get drinks, she felt vulnerable, alone. She kept her eyes focused on the floor, trying to be quiet and invisible, as if facing wild animals. If they didn't notice her, they might not tear her to shreds with their teeth and claws.

It didn't work.

Within moments, three former debutantes blocked her like bouncers at a bar.

"Well, well, well." A skinny young woman in a designer gown gave her a hard-edged smile. "Letitia Spencer. This is a surprise. Isn't it, Caroline?"

"A big surprise."

Letty vaguely recognized the two women from her school, where they'd been a year older. They were looking at her now with the cold expressions of mob enforcers. She could suddenly imagine how her father must have felt right before that thug had broken his arm.

But the third woman stood a slight distance

from the first two. It was Poppy Alexander. She and Letty had once been study partners, sophomore year. Poppy just stood there, looking pale and uneasy.

"Excuse me." Letty backed away. "I don't want any trouble."

"You don't want trouble?" The first woman's lip twisted scornfully. "How very amusing."

"Amusing," Caroline echoed with a sneer.

"You shouldn't be here."

"You're a disgrace to society."

"If you had any decency, you'd disappear or die."

Poppy stood silently beside her friends, looking faintly sick, as if she wished she were a million miles away. Letty sympathized with that feeling.

The first woman continued with a sneer, "You might think you're safe on Darius Kyrillos's arm, but…"

"Ah, there you are, Letty," Darius said smoothly, coming up behind them. "I brought your drink." Turning to the other women, he gave a charming smile. "Ah. Augusta. Caroline. And Poppy Alexander. How lovely to see you."

"Hello, Darius," they cooed with weak smiles, then departed, the first two with a final venomous glance at Letty, Poppy hanging her head, looking guilty and ashamed.

Emotions Letty knew well.

"Everything all right?" Darius murmured after they left.

She exhaled, blinking fast. "Fine. Just fine."

The night only got worse. It was past ten when the formal dinner was finally served, and Letty felt half-starved as she sat down beside Darius at the prestigious head table. But as she felt the glares from the four other couples at the table, she could barely eat a bite of salad or the lobster with white truffle cream. At any moment, she half expected one of the hedge fund millionaires or society wives might smash a three-hundred-dollar champagne bottle against the table and attack her with it.

That might have been preferable to the waves of unspoken hatred overtaking her like a blast of heat from all sides. During the unendurably long meal, Darius tried several times to start conversations with the others at the table. Each time, he succeeded. Until he tried to include her. Then the conversation instantly died.

Finally, Letty could stand it no longer.

"Excuse me," she breathed, rising from her seat. "I have to—"

She couldn't finish her sentence. Turning, she rushed past all the other tables and out of the ballroom. Going down the long hall, she found a ladies' bathroom, where she was violently sick. Going to the sink, she washed out her mouth. She looked at herself wanly in the mirror. She felt like she'd rather die than go back into that ballroom and see Darius trying to stick up for her.

Better for her to just leave quietly. Better for both of them.

After lingering as long as she could in the cool quiet of the empty, marble bathroom, with the old-fashioned elegance of a more genteel era, she went out into the hallway.

She found Darius waiting for her, smolderingly handsome in his tuxedo, leaning against the wall with his arms folded and his jaw tight.

"Are you all right?"

He was angry. She could hear it in his voice. She stopped, barely holding back her tears. "Have you seen enough?" she choked out. "You're surely not enough of an idiot to marry me."

He came closer in the empty hallway, with its plush carpets and gold light fixtures. She tensed, waiting for him to tell her he'd obviously made a mistake, bringing her to his ball, and that there was no way he would marry her now or in fact ever wanted to see her again. She waited for him to give her what she'd wanted and set her free.

Except in this moment the thought didn't make her as happy as it once did.

He narrowed his eyes. "I didn't realize how bad it was for you."

She'd successfully fought back tears all night. But she could do it no longer. Not now, when the illusion of having a protector—even for a night— was coming to an end.

Letty took a deep breath, trying to ignore the

lump in her throat, wiping her eyes before he'd see the tears. She tried to smile. "But now you know. So tomorrow I'll go to Rochester with my father. You can continue to be rich and famous and popular here. You can visit our baby anytime you want…" Something in his eyes made her voice trail off uncertainly. "If you even want to see our baby anymore," she whispered.

His eyes suddenly blazed with cold fury. "No."

"What?"

He gripped her arm. "I said no."

She tried to pull away, but couldn't. "What are you doing?"

"What I should have done the moment we arrived here."

He pulled her grimly down the hall, back toward the ballroom.

"No," she choked out, struggling. "Please. I can't go back in there. Don't make me…"

Darius was merciless. He dragged her back into the enormous ballroom, with its high ceiling and crystal chandeliers. He gripped her wrist as she limped behind him in the tight stiletto shoes and pink dress, going past all the big round tables, where a thousand people were now drinking after-dinner brandies and coffees and the men, at least, were eating desserts. Letty felt each ten-person table fall silent as they went by. She felt everyone's judgment. Their blame. Their hatred.

Ruthlessly, Darius pulled her through the ballroom, leaving people silent in their wake. As he walked past their own table, he grabbed his glass of champagne. Crossing the small dance floor, he dragged her up the stairs to the stage, where, still holding her wrist, he took the microphone at the podium. He cleared his throat.

Letty's knees were trembling with fear. She wished she'd never come here—wished she'd never taken a single risk—would have given twenty years of her life to be back at her tiny apartment, snug on the sofa with a blanket over her head!

"Good evening," Darius said into the microphone. His husky, commanding voice rang over the ballroom. A spotlight fell on him. "For those of you I haven't yet met personally, I'm Darius Kyrillos. Thank you for coming to my party, the event kicking off the New York fall social season, and thank you for supporting scholarships for kids in need. It's because of you that many deserving youngsters will be able to go to college or learn a trade."

A smattering of applause ensued; much less enthusiastic than it would have been if Letty hadn't been standing with him on stage. She was ruining everything, she thought unhappily. Even for those kids who needed help. She hated herself. Almost as much as she hated him.

Darius deliberately turned away from the microphone to give her a searching glance, and her stomach fell to the floor. *Here it comes*, she thought. *He's going to announce that he brought me here as a joke and have me thrown me out.* She was social poison, so he really had no choice but to distance himself. This was exactly what she'd expected.

She just hadn't expected it to hurt so much when it happened.

Darius's lips twisted. He turned back to the microphone. "Most of you know this beautiful woman on stage with me. Miss Letitia Spencer." There was a low hiss across the ballroom, a rumble of muffled booing. He responded with a charming smile. "Since we're all friends, I wanted you to be the first to know...I just asked her to marry me."

Letty's eyes went wide. What? Why would he say that? Was he insane?

"And she has accepted," he finished calmly. "So I want you all to be the first to wish us joy."

This time, the gasp came from Letty. Forget insane. Was he suicidal?

The low hisses and boos changed to ugly muttering across the ballroom, angry, obscene words that made Letty squirm. Instinctively, she covered her belly with her arms to protect her unborn baby from the cruel words.

But Darius's smile only widened as he put his large hand over hers, on her belly.

"We're expecting a baby, too. All of this has left me so overwhelmed with joy, I want to share it with all of you. Now. Some of you might know of her father's troubles…"

A white-haired man, unable to contain himself any longer, sprang up from his table. "Howard Spencer defrauded my company of millions of dollars!" he cried, shaking his fist. "We were only repaid a fraction of what we lost!"

A low buzz of rage hummed around him.

"Letty's father is a criminal," Darius agreed. "He abused your trust, and I know over half of what he stole is still unaccounted for. But *Letty* did nothing wrong. Her only crime was loving a father who didn't deserve it. That's why I've decided, in my future bride's honor, to make amends."

Suddenly, it was dead quiet across the tables.

Darius held his champagne glass high. "I will personally pay back every penny her father stole."

A collective gasp ripped through the ballroom.

The white-haired man staggered back. "But that's…*five billion dollars!*"

"So it is," Darius said mildly. He looked over the crowd. "So if your family is still owed money by Howard Spencer, I personally guarantee repayment. All in honor of my beautiful…innocent… unfairly hounded…bride." Turning back toward Letty on stage, he held up his champagne glass and said into the microphone, "To Letitia Spencer!"

As photographers rushed forward, Letty felt faint. Camera flashes lit up everywhere. There was a rumble of noise, of shouts and gasps and chairs hastily pushed aside as a thousand people scrambled to their feet and lifted their champagne glasses into the air.

"Letitia Spencer!" they cried joyfully.

CHAPTER SEVEN

IT WASN'T EVERY day a man spent five billion dollars on a whim.

Darius hadn't intended to do it. He'd had a different surprise in mind for Letty tonight: a black velvet box hidden in the pocket of his tuxedo jacket, which he'd planned to spring on her as soon as the evening was over and all her overblown fears had proved unfounded.

Instead, he'd realized how much she'd endured over the last ten years. Alone. While he'd been happily free to live an anonymous life and make his fortune.

Standing in the hallway, when he'd seen her come out of the bathroom looking shattered and as pale as a ghost, he'd finally realized the toll it had taken on her. And if this was how people treated Letty now, how much worse had it been ten years ago, when their rage had been white-hot?

He'd been forced to ask himself: If Letty had actually shown up the night they were going to run away together and told him about her father's confession, what would have happened?

Darius would have of course insisted she marry

him anyway. After all, what did her father's stupid investment fund have to do with their love?

But as her husband, he would have been at her side throughout the scandal and media circus of a trial. He might not have received the critical early loan that enabled him to build his software, to hire employees, to lease his first office space. He would have been too tainted by association as Howard Spencer's son-in-law.

If Letty hadn't set him free, he might have been unemployable, unable to easily provide for his wife or children. He might be living in that tiny Brooklyn apartment, too, struggling with the loss of his dreams. Struggling to provide for his family. Struggling not to feel like a failure as a man.

It was Letty's sacrifice ten years ago that had made his current success possible.

While he'd been triumphantly building his billion-dollar company, she'd lived in poverty, suffering endless humiliations for a crime that wasn't even hers. And she'd kept her sacrifice a secret, so he'd never once had to feel guilty about deserting her.

Even now, she continued to protect him. She'd warned him what would happen if he brought her as his date. And now he'd finally seen how the members of the so-called upper class had treated her all this time. He'd watched Letty bear their insults without complaint. And he'd realized her stigma was so bad that, in spite of his arrogant earlier assumption, his presence alone wasn't enough to shelter her.

He knew how it felt to be treated badly.

He'd once been the poorest child in his village, mocked as an unloved bastard. He was now the most beloved, feared man of Heraklios. He did pretty well in Manhattan, too. And London. And Paris and Rome, Sydney and Tokyo.

Money could buy everything from houses to souls.

Money made the man.

It astonished him that not everyone realized this. Some people seemed to think love was the most important thing. They were either fools, Darius thought grimly, or gluttons for punishment. He'd learned his own lesson well. The sick truth was that love only led to pain.

Love was a pale facsimile of money. Love begged.

Money demanded.

So when Darius had seen how badly New York society had treated Letty for all these years—these people who didn't have a fraction of her kindness or her loyalty or her heart—ice had seized his soul.

Especially when he'd realized that he'd treated her even worse. After a decade of ignoring her, he'd taken revenge for her so-called sins through cold seduction, insults and threats.

His jaw tightened. He would pay that debt.

Darius didn't love her. The part of his heart that

had once craved love had been burned away. Love wasn't something he ever wanted to feel for anyone.

But there were other qualities Darius did believe in.

Honor.

Loyalty.

Protecting his woman.

So he'd settled the matter, once and for all.

Now Letty would be the most popular girl in the city. Every person who'd once treated her shabbily would be begging for an invitation to their wedding. Begging to be her friend.

At the moment of Darius's triumph, as he toasted her on stage, he turned to face Letty at the podium. Rough, raw desire surged through his body as he looked at her—his woman now, *his*—lush and pregnant and obscenely beautiful in that pink gown, which slid over her breasts and belly like a caress.

She stood unsteadily in those ridiculous stiletto heels, beneath the blinding spotlight, as a thousand people applauded from the darkness. People who had treated her like garbage just minutes before started chanting her name. Camera flashes lit up the darkness as reporters shouted questions.

"Miss Spencer, what's it like to be loved to the tune of five billion dollars?"

"When's the wedding?"

"When's your baby due?"

"How does it feel to suddenly be the most popular girl in New York?"

Letty looked at Darius with the expression of a terrified deer, and he realized she wasn't enjoying this as much as he was.

Turning back to the microphone with a smile, Darius answered for her. "The wedding will be soon. No plans yet. Our baby will be born soon, too." He looked past the reporters to the well-heeled crowd. "That's all. Thank you for your support! Enjoy your night. And since you're now all so much richer, don't forget to be generous to the scholarship fund—it's for the kids." Setting his empty champagne glass on the podium, he glanced at the full orchestra. "Let's start the music!"

"Kick off the dancing, Darius!" someone shouted from the back.

"Yes, the first dance to you and Letty!" someone else cried.

Darius led her down the steps from the stage, and as they reached the dance floor, the music started, a slow, romantic song he'd purposefully requested from the orchestra earlier because he knew Letty would remember it from that long-ago summer.

He was right. She stopped when she heard it, eyes wide.

Darius looked down at her with a crooked half smile. "What do you say? Will you dance with me, Letty?"

She looked around at all the people who had treated her with such contempt for the last ten years, now beaming at her as if they were best friends.

"Why are they acting as if they like me?" she said softly, for his ears alone.

"People love to talk about character and loyalty and love. They mean money." He allowed himself a grim smile. "Now the money's been paid, so they can love you again."

Letty's head snapped back to look at him. Her big hazel eyes, fringed with dark lashes, were wide, as if he were a superhero who'd flown down from the sky. "Why did you do it, Darius? Why pay five billion dollars for a debt that isn't yours?"

The music swirled around them like a whirlwind. "Do you remember our old waltz?"

Her forehead creased. "Of course..." She looked back at the people yelling encouragement for them to dance. She bit her lip. "But not in front of everyone..."

"Now." Darius pulled her against his tuxedo-clad body. "Dance with me."

Letty's long dark hair was falling softly around her beautiful face to her shoulders, nestling against the diamonds sparkling around her neck. He'd already wanted her, but as he felt her body in his arms, and the crush of her belly and swollen breasts against his chest, he wanted her even more.

Just like that long-ago summer...

"Come on, Letty," he said in a low voice. "Let's show them all we don't give a damn."

He moved commandingly onto the dance floor, leading her in the first steps of the waltz he'd helped her practice for her debutante ball long ago, the spring of her senior year. They'd practiced the waltz over and over in the sunlit spring flower meadow on the Fairholme estate, overlooking the sparkling bay, as music sang from her phone.

They'd started out as friends and ended as something else entirely.

When she'd left for her debutante ball in Manhattan that May, looking beautiful beyond belief in her white dress, Darius spent the whole evening prowling the meadow in a rage, hating the Harvard boy who was her date.

He'd been shocked when Letty came back early, whispering, "I didn't want to dance with anyone but you…"

Darius had taken one look at Letty's joyous, upturned face surrounded by spring flowers, and then he, the chauffeur's son, had done the unthinkable: he'd wrapped her in his powerful arms and kissed her…

Now, as he swirled her around in that waltz, it was like going back in time. The audience standing on the edge of the dance floor clapped their approval. In this moment, in this place, Darius and Letty were the king and queen of the city, the pinnacle of all his youthful dreams.

But he barely noticed the crowds. There was only Letty. He was back in that meadow, a young man so sure of his own heart, so naively enthusiastic about his future, dancing with the beautiful princess he'd dreamed about, the one he could never deserve. And, oh, how he'd craved her to his very core…

Now, Darius pulled her more indecently close to his hard, aching body than any waltz allowed. She lifted her luminous gaze to his, visibly holding her breath. The electricity between them suddenly sizzled with heat.

He stopped dancing. Louder than the music, he heard the rush of his blood in his ears, the pounding of his own heart.

He needed her in his bed.

Now.

The music abruptly ended, and the ballroom exploded in applause echoing from the high ceiling. Without a word, Darius led her from the dance floor. He pulled her through the crowds, which parted for them like magic. Compliments and cheers followed them. Everywhere, people were apologizing to Letty for how badly they'd treated her. He recognized Poppy Alexander.

"I'm so sorry, Letty," the girl blurted out. "I was afraid to be your friend. I knew it wasn't your fault, what happened, but I was a coward…"

"That's all right, Poppy," Letty replied gently.

She looked around at everyone else. "I don't blame anyone."

Darius thought about the dragon Poppy had for a mother, and he couldn't blame her for being scared. Until he thought of how bad Letty's life had been for the last decade, and he didn't think any of them deserved another minute of Letty's time.

He swept Letty away without looking back. He didn't care about anyone or anything right now, except getting her into his bed.

Darius pulled his phone from his tuxedo jacket pocket. By the time they exited the stately beaux-arts building, his limo was waiting at the curb. Collins leaped out and opened the passenger door.

The second they were in the backseat, and the door closed behind them, Darius pulled Letty roughly into his arms and kissed her.

Her lips were sweet as sin. She trembled, her curves melting against him. His whole body was hard with need. He had to have her.

"Sir?" said Collins from the driver's seat.

"Home," he said hoarsely. "As fast as you can."

Then he pressed the button that raised the barrier between front and back seats. Just those few seconds were agony. But he was not willing to share Letty with anyone. He'd shared her enough.

She belonged to him now. To him alone.

Once they had privacy in the backseat, he kissed her passionately as the limo moved through the sparkling streets of the lit-up city at midnight. But all he could see was her sensual beauty. All he could feel was the soft brush of her long dark hair, and her warm skin like silk beneath his hands. He pushed her back against the leather seat, devouring her soft lips, kissing her neck, running his hands over her full breasts overflowing the tight pink bodice of her dress.

He kissed her savagely, biting and sucking her lower lip. A gasp of need came from her throat as she returned his kiss with matching fire, gripping his shoulders through his tuxedo jacket. He kissed slowly down her neck as her head fell back, her eyes closed, her expression one of ecstasy.

When he saw that, it was all he could do not to take her, right here in the back of the limo. He was unconsciously reaching for his fly when he realized they'd stopped.

Resurfacing from his haze of desire, he saw the limo was parked beneath the porte cochere in front of his building. Just in time, too. He glanced at Letty, stretched back against the smooth calf-skin leather seat. Her big hazel eyes were smoky with passion, her dark hair mussed, her pink dress disheveled. Another moment and he would have yanked up her dress and roughly pushed inside her.

That wasn't how he wanted this night to be, fast and brutish in the back of a limo. No. After the disaster of their first night together, when he'd taken her virginity then insulted her and tossed her out of the penthouse into the snow, he wanted this night to be perfect.

He would finally treat Letitia Spencer, the forbidden princess of his youth, as she deserved to be treated.

He would enjoy her as he deserved to enjoy her. *Thoroughly.*

Reaching over, he smoothed the fabric of Letty's bodice modestly back over her breasts just as the passenger door opened behind him.

Taking her hand, he led her out of the limo and into the elegant lobby, where the doorman greeted him. "Good evening, sir."

"Good evening, Jones." Such civilized words. Wearing a tuxedo, Darius knew he must appear civilized on the outside. On the inside, he felt anything but.

Gripping Letty's hand, he desperately kept himself in check. Neither of them looked at each other as they went through the high-ceilinged lobby, past the front desk to the elevator. Civilized.

But as soon as the door closed behind them, they were in each other's arms. He pushed her against the wall, kissing her hungrily, desperately.

She breathed against his skin, "I still can't believe you're doing this."

"Kissing you?"

"Giving five billion dollars away. Why did you do it?"

"Don't you know?" he growled, his lips against hers. "Can't you guess?"

Panting, she shook her head. "You hate my father..."

Darius's lip curled as he drew back. "I didn't do it for him."

"For your friends?"

"Those aren't my friends."

"For the other victims, then. All those hardworking people with pensions. Firemen. Nurses..."

"I'm not that noble."

The elevator door opened. The floor-to-ceiling windows flooded the penthouse with moonlight. Taking her hand, he led her inside. He could hear the tap of her stiletto heels against the marble.

She stopped, staring up at him.

"Then why?" she whispered.

"I couldn't stand to see you treated badly," Darius said huskily, "when all you've done is give your love and loyalty to someone who doesn't deserve it."

She bit her lip. "I know my father isn't perfect—"

"Perfect?" His jaw tightened. "He's a criminal—" He cut himself off, then said, "You're under my protection now."

She looked troubled. "Your protection—or your rule?"

"It is the same. I protect what is mine."

"Our baby."

His eyes met hers. "And you."

Letty stared at him, her eyes wide, as if she had no idea how to react. As if she had forgotten what it was like to have anyone properly look after her.

He wondered how long it had been since anyone had tried to take care of her, rather than the other way around. He suspected Letty always sacrificed herself to take care of others—especially that father of hers—while her own heart bled.

"But I'm not yours," she said quietly. "Not truly. We got pregnant by accident. I didn't think you were serious about marriage."

"I am."

"That commitment is serious, Darius. It means... forever."

"I know," he said.

She swallowed, searching his gaze. "I was sure after tonight you'd never want to see me again."

Taking her hand, he lifted it slowly to his lips. She seemed to hold her breath, watching as he kissed the back of her hand, breathing against her skin. Straightening, he held her hand tightly in his own. "I want to see you tomorrow, and every other tomorrow for the rest of our lives."

"Darius..."

"You will marry me, Letty," he said in a low voice. "You know it, and I know it. In your heart, you were always meant to be mine."

Marry him? For real?

How could she?

Even if Darius no longer hated her, he certainly didn't love her. And she was starting to fear she could love him again. Perhaps all too easily.

What hope could they have of happiness?

He'd never love her back. All he wished to do was possess her. He offered sex and money, and in return, he'd expect sex and total devotion. For her, those things went together. He wouldn't have just her body, but her soul.

So why was she still so tempted?

She shivered, caught between fear and desire.

"Are you cold?" he asked huskily, his eyes dark.

"No, I…I…" Hugging her baby bump, she gasped, "I need some fresh air."

He smiled. "Come with me."

Still holding her hand, he led her through the moon-bathed penthouse, and she thought dimly how she was getting in the habit of following where he led. But with his hand enveloping hers so protectively, she didn't want to do anything else.

She still couldn't believe what he'd done, announcing their engagement, defending her in front of all those people—and then telling the world he intended to pay billions of dollars of his own money to repay what her father had stolen.

She'd been dazed. Then she'd danced with him, the same routine he'd helped her learn so long ago, and she'd been back in that spring meadow, practicing the waltz not for the pimply-faced Harvard boy, who was the nephew of her father's lawyer, but for Darius, always for him, only for him. As they'd danced in the ballroom, she'd felt time melt away.

Darius was right. She was his. From the very beginning, Darius Kyrillos had been the only man she'd ever wanted. The only man she'd ever loved.

I don't love him anymore, she told herself desperately. She wouldn't let him buy her!

Darius led her up an elaborate staircase, then pushed open a glass door that led out onto a private rooftop garden.

Letty gasped at the beauty of the ivy-covered pergola decorated with fairy lights near a lit lap pool gleaming bright blue in the warm September night.

Above them, distant stars sparkled like diamonds across a dark velvety sky. Past the glass walls of the terrace, the night skyline of Manhattan glittered.

She kept her distance from the edge, afraid to go too close. But Darius went right to it. He leaned against the short glass wall, totally unfazed and unafraid of plummeting seventy floors to his death. He looked out at the city.

Letty crept closer, her heart pounding. "This terrace is amazing."

"All the flowers remind me of home," he said simply. She wondered if he meant Greece or Fairholme, but didn't have the nerve to ask. She slowly turned her head, marveling at the lavish beauty of a rooftop garden that treated all of Manhattan as nothing but a backdrop.

"You're king of the mountain now," she said softly. "Looking down on a valley of skyscrapers."

Turning to her, he came forward. Then he abruptly fell to one knee in front of her astonished eyes.

Reaching into his tuxedo jacket pocket, he pulled out a small black velvet box.

"Rule it with me, Letty," he said quietly. "As my wife."

Shivering, she put her hand on her heart. "I already said…"

"You said yes when you thought I'd back out. This is a real proposal. I expect a real answer." He held up the black velvet box. "Letty Spencer, will you do me the honor of marrying me?"

He opened the lid. Inside the black velvet box was an enormous pear-shaped diamond set in platinum. It was the hugest, most outrageous ring she'd ever seen.

But that wasn't what made her lose her breath.

It was Darius's face. His dark, yearning eyes. As he looked at her in the moonlight, she saw the man who'd just bruised her with the intensity of his kisses. Who'd just defied all of Manhattan and paid five billion dollars for her. The man whose child she carried.

In his eyes, she saw the shadow of the younger man she'd once loved, strong and kind, with such a good heart. The one who'd loved her so fervently. *They were the same.*

Letty's heart skipped a beat.

It's an illusion, she told herself desperately. *He's not the same.* But as she reached out and brushed her fingers against the diamond engagement ring, it sparkled like the stars. Like the lights of this powerful city.

Like the smolder in Darius's dark eyes.

"It would destroy us," she said shakily, but what she really meant was *it would destroy me.*

Darius slowly rose in front of her, until his tall, powerful body towered over hers. Waves of blue light from the pool reflected against him as the warm wind moved across the water. Putting his hand on her cheek, he lowered his head.

"Say yes," he whispered. "Say you'll be mine."

His kiss was tender at first. She felt the rough warmth of his lips, the gentle hold of his arms.

Then his grip tightened. His embrace became hungry, filled with need. Spirals of heat twisted through her body, and she gripped his shoulders. Until he pulled away.

"Say it," he demanded.

"Yes," she choked out.

A flash of triumph crossed his starkly handsome face. "You will?"

She nodded, tears in her eyes.

"There will be no going back," he warned.

"I know." She tried to ignore the thrill that crept into her heart. Excitement? Terror?

Right or wrong, disaster or not, there was nothing to be done. What he'd said was true. She'd always been his. In many ways, this decision had been made for her long ago.

He slid the diamond ring over the third finger of her left hand. It fit perfectly. She looked down at it, sparkling in the moonlight. "How did you know my ring size?"

"It's the same ring."

She frowned. "What?"

"It's the same I bought for you ten years ago." His voice was low. "I had it set with a different stone."

The thought that he'd kept their original ring all these years made her heart ache. Whatever he might say, didn't that mean he might still care for her, at least a little?

Could love, once lost, ever be regained?

Looking at him with tears in her eyes, she breathed, "Darius…"

"You're mine now, Letty," he whispered, kissing her forehead, her eyelids, her cheeks. "You belong to me. Forever."

Then he kissed her lips as if those, too, were his possession.

Sparks of pleasure went up and down Letty's body, coiling low and deep inside her, and she felt his hands running down her bare arms, her sides, cupping her breasts over the pink dress.

She fell back against the ivy-covered stone wall. Above them, fairy lights swayed gently in the warm wind, the skyscrapers of Manhattan illuminating the moonlit sky.

Letty's eyes closed as he kissed his way down her throat. She felt breathless, like she was lost in a dream.

He kissed over the diamond necklace to her bare clavicle and the valley between her full breasts, half revealed above the low-cut bodice of her gown.

Picking her up, he carried her past the sweeping ivy into a half-enclosed room protected on two sides by walls, with a rustic chandelier hanging over a long table. Two leather sofas were arranged around a fireplace and well-stocked bar.

He flicked a switch, and the gas fire lit up. She saw Darius's face clearly in the flickering firelight as they faced each other silently. The soft wind blew against her hair, her skin.

Slowly, Darius removed his tuxedo jacket and dropped it to the flagstone floor. Coming closer, he unzipped her pink dress. She felt the brush of his fingertips, then the warm night air against her bare skin as her gown dropped to the floor beside his jacket. She stepped out of the fabric, wearing only the diamonds, a lace bra, panties and the wicked pink crystal stiletto heels.

He stepped back, looking at her.

"Incredible," he breathed in deep masculine appreciation, and she realized that, just as he'd promised, he was seeing her in the lingerie. She scowled.

"Do you always get what you want?" she said accusingly.

"I do," he said, caressing her cheek. "And now, so will you."

She licked her lips and felt a thrill of delight as his expression changed to raw desire. Reaching up, she saucily loosened his tuxedo tie, before tugging on it, drawing him closer for a kiss.

It was the first time she'd ever made the first move, and he growled fierce approval. Holding her tight, he kissed her back hungrily.

His hands caressed her naked skin, her arms, her shoulders, the small of her back. And suddenly she couldn't remove his clothes fast enough. His tie, cuff links, shirt. They all dropped to the floor.

His tanned body, laced with dark hair, looked like sculpted marble in the flickering firelight, all hard muscles and taut belly. She brushed her hand lightly against his chest. His skin felt like silk over steel. Biting her lip, she lifted her eyes to his.

"If I'm yours, Darius," she whispered, standing in front of him in the half-enclosed room, "you're mine."

Brushing back long dark tendrils of her hair, he pulled her roughly into his arms. His hard-muscled chest moved against her full, aching breasts and pregnant belly. The soft wind whispered against her bare skin as he unhooked her silk lace bra, and her breasts sprang free. He looked down at her body and gave a quick breath.

Pressing her breasts together, he cupped their weight in his hands before he lowered his head to suckle one pink, full nipple, then the other.

Shuddering with pleasure, she closed her eyes.

His hands stroked gently, reverently, down her body to her naked belly to her hips, still covered with the tiny silk panties.

Running his hand down her legs, he knelt before her and pulled off one stiletto, then the other, as she balanced against him, her hands gripping his shoulders. She remained standing—barely—as he caressed upward from her manicured toes, to the tender hollows of her knees, and higher still. She swallowed, holding her breath as he stroked up her thighs.

She closed her eyes, heart pounding as he pulled her panties down her legs. She couldn't move fast enough. He impatiently ripped them off in his powerful hands, tossing the flimsy silk aside.

"Those were expensive—" she protested.

He looked up, and the edges of his cruel, sensual mouth curved upward. "They served their purpose."

An icy fear suddenly crept through her heart as Letty wondered if she, too, might someday have served her purpose. If he might someday rip her apart, then discard her.

Then all her rational thought fled as, still on his knees, he gripped her hips and moved between her legs.

She felt the warmth of his breath on the most sensitive, intimate part of her body, as she stood naked with the warm night breeze swirling against her skin, as one of New York's most famous billionaires knelt before her in the firelight, beneath the ivy walls of a rooftop garden.

Holding her tight, he lowered his mouth between her thighs and tasted her with a soft moan. He licked her as if she were a melting ice cream cone in his favorite flavor, creamy and sweet. As she gasped, his rhythm intensified, until he worked her with his tongue, sliding sensuously against her. Pleasure exploded through her body almost immediately, and he gripped her hips, keeping her firmly against his mouth as her body twisted with the sudden intensity of pleasure that left her knees weak and sent spasms all over her body.

She was still dizzy in the heights of pleasure as he rose to his feet and drew her toward the sofa. He lay down first, stretching out naked against the black leather, hard and ready for her. She took a step, then hesitated, biting her lip.

"What is it?"

She tried not to look at how huge he was, his

hard shaft jutting arrogantly from his body. She blushed, feeling shy. "Um, what do I do?"

He gave a low, lazy laugh, then pulled her over him.

"I'll show you," he said huskily.

He spread her across him on the sofa, her thighs over his hips, his arousal pressing low against her pregnant belly. He reached up, cupping her cheek. As he drew her down for a kiss, her long dark hair fell like a veil against his skin.

The kiss was tender at first. She relaxed into it with a sigh, her body curving over his as his hands roamed gently over her back, her arms, her belly, her breasts. Then his kiss deepened, turning urgent and fierce. Placing his hands on her hips, he lifted her up, positioning himself beneath her.

He slowly lowered her down on him, filling her, inch by delicious inch, in tantalizing slow motion.

She gasped as she felt him inside her, going deep, then deeper still. Her whole body started to tighten, more savagely than it had before.

Lifting her hips, he lowered her again, showing her the rhythm, until her body started to move of its own accord. Closing her eyes with fervent intensity, she rode him, slowly at first, then faster. The pleasure built and built...

Her lips parted in a silent cry as joy burst like fireworks shaking through her body. She heard his low gasp as he, too, exploded, pouring inside her.

She collapsed, falling softly against him on the black leather sofa.

For long moments, he held her tenderly, as if her weight were nothing. Their bodies were still fused, slick with sweat, as he leaned up to kiss her. He felt so solid and strong beneath her. Like a foundation that could never be shaken.

She shivered in his arms. In the half-enclosed outdoor room, the September night was growing cool. But that wasn't the reason.

The idea of being Darius's wife had seemed like a recipe for disaster, if not outright doom. And so it would be, if she were tempted into giving him her heart, while in return, he gave her only money.

Letty looked down at the heavy diamond ring, now shining dully on her left hand.

If only Darius could again be the young man she remembered, with the kind nature and forgiving heart. She would willingly give him everything. Not just her body, not just her name, but her heart.

CHAPTER EIGHT

HE WAS A GENIUS, Darius thought as he woke in his bed the next morning with sunlight flooding in through the windows. He looked down at Letty sleeping beside him and smiled. A damn genius. Best five billion dollars ever spent.

And he would spend the rest of his life being thrilled, if it continued paying off like it did last night. The sex had been spectacular. And even more. Something had changed in the way Letty looked at him. He loved the mixture of gratitude and shy hope he saw in her eyes.

He kissed Letty's temple tenderly. She yawned, stretching like a cat.

"What time is it?" she murmured, her eyes still closed.

"Late," he said, amused. "Almost noon."

Her eyes flew open. "Oh, no! I'm late for—" Then she seemed to remember how much had changed in the last twenty-four hours, and that being late for work was no longer an issue. "Oh. Right." She bit her lip, blushing and looking so adorable that he was tempted to keep her in bed another hour.

It was incredible how much he still wanted her,

when they'd made love *four times* last night—on the rooftop terrace, here in bed, and in the shower when they decided to wash off. Only to promptly get all sweaty again when they returned to bed.

Letty was meant to be his, Darius marveled. He'd never felt so sexually satisfied in his life.

And yet already he wanted more. How was it possible?

He smiled down at her. "Hungry?"

"Starving," she admitted. "And thirsty."

"I can solve that." Rising from the bed, he got a white terry cloth robe and handed her one, too. "Come out to the kitchen."

She gave a sudden scowl, and even that was adorable. "You didn't tell me you had staff staying at the penthouse. What if they heard us last night? What if they—"

"There are no live-in staff. I have a housekeeper who comes in four times a week, that's it."

She blinked in confusion. "Then who's going to cook?"

"I'm not totally useless."

She looked at him with unflattering shock in her eyes. "You can't cook, Darius."

"No?" His smile widened to a grin. "Come see."

She ate her words shortly afterward, sitting in the brightly lit kitchen at the counter, as he served her an omelet to order with tomatoes, bacon and five kinds of cheese, along with orange juice over ice. When she took the first bite of the omelet, her eyes went wide.

"Good, huh?" he said smugly, sitting beside her with his own enormous omelet of ham and cheese, drenched in salsa. Being a sexual hero all night definitely had built his appetite.

And hers, as well. If he felt like a hero, Letty was a sex *goddess*, he thought. Even now, he felt aware of her, just sitting companionably beside her at the counter with its dazzling view of the city through floor-to-ceiling windows. But he wasn't looking at the view. He was watching her.

"Delicious," she moaned softly as she gobbled it down, bite after bite. "We should serve omelets at our wedding."

He gave a low laugh. "I appreciate the compliment, but I don't see myself whipping up omelets for a thousand."

She froze. "A thousand? *Guests?*"

Gulping black coffee, he shrugged. "Our wedding will be the social event of the year, as you deserve. All of New York society will come and grovel at your feet."

She didn't look thrilled. She took another bite of omelet. "That's not what I want."

"No?" he said lazily, tucking back a tendril of her dark hair. His eyes traced the creamy skin of her neck, down to the smooth temptation of her clavicle and swell of her breasts above the luxurious white cotton robe. He glanced down to her belt, tied loosely between her breasts and pregnant belly. He had the sudden impulse to sweep all the dishes to the floor, tug open her robe and lean her back naked against the counter.

"A wedding should be a happy occasion." She shook her head. "Those society people aren't my friends. They never really were. Why would I invite them?"

"To rub your new status in their faces? I thought you'd glory in your return to status as the queen of it all."

"Me?" Letty snorted. "I was never queen of anything. As a teenager I never knew the right clothes to wear or understood how to play the society game. I was a total nerd."

He frowned. "I never saw you that way. I just assumed…"

"That I was a spoiled princess?" She gave him a funny smile. "I *was* spoiled, though not the way you mean. I always knew I was loved." Her face was wistful. "My parents loved each other and they loved me."

Revenge wasn't Letty's style, Darius realized. She never showed off or tried to make others feel bad. Even when she was younger, she'd always been most comfortable reading the dusty leather-bound books in Fairholme's oak-paneled library, baking cakes with the cook in the kitchen or playing with the gardener's kittens in the yard. Letty never wanted to be the center of attention. She was always more worried about other people's feelings than her own.

In this respect, Darius thought, the two of them were very different.

"And I had a real home," she whispered.

Memories of that beautiful gray stone manor on the edge of the sea, surrounded by roses, came to his mind. He said gruffly, "You still miss Fairholme after all this time?"

She gave him a sad smile. "I know it's gone for good. But I still dream about it. My mother was born there. Four generations of my family."

"What happened to it?"

She looked down at her plate. "A tech billionaire bought it at a cut-rate price. I heard he changed everything, added zebra-print shag carpeting and neon lights, and turned the nursery into his own private disco. Of course that was his right. But he wouldn't let me take a picture of my great-grandmother's fresco before he destroyed it with his sandblaster."

A low growl came from Darius's throat. He remembered the nursery fresco, a charming monstrosity picturing a sad-eyed little goose girl leading ducks and geese through what looked like a Bavarian village. Not his cup of tea, but it was part of the house's history. "I'm sorry."

She looked up with a bright, fake smile. "It's fine. Of course it couldn't last. Good things never do."

"Neither do bad things," he said quietly. "Nothing lasts, good or bad."

"I guess you're right." She wrapped her arms around her pregnant belly. "But I don't want a big society wedding, Darius. I think I'd just like you and me, and our closest family and friends. I don't need ten bridesmaids. I just want one."

"An old friend?"

She smiled. "A new one. Belle Langtry. A waitress at the diner. How about you? Who would you choose as your best man?"

"Ángel Velazquez."

"Ángel?"

"It's a nickname. His real first name is Santiago, but he hates it, because he was named after a man who refused to recognize him as his son."

"How awful!"

Darius shrugged. "I call him by his last name. Velazquez hates weddings. He recently had to be the best man for a friend of ours, Kassius Black. He complained for months. All that tender love gave him a headache, he said."

Letty was looking at him in dismay. "And you want him at our wedding?"

"He needs a little torture. When you meet him you'll see what I mean. Completely arrogant, always sure he's right."

"Hard to imagine," she said drily.

"So Velazquez. And my extended family."

Her eyes brightened. "Your family?"

"My great-aunt, Theia Ioanna, who lives in Athens. Assorted uncles, aunts and cousins, and the rest of my village on Heraklios, the island I'm from."

"Could we bring them all over from Greece? And of course we'll have my father…"

Darius stiffened. "No."

"No?" She frowned. "We could get married on Heraklios, if they can't travel. I've always wanted to visit the Greek islands…"

"I mean your father. He's not invited."

"Of course he's invited. He's my father. He'll walk me down the aisle. I know you don't like him, but he's my only family."

"Letty, I thought you understood." His jaw was taut, his voice low and cold. "I don't want you, or our baby, within ten feet of that man ever again."

"What?"

"It's not negotiable." Swiveling to face her at the counter, Darius gripped her shoulder. "I will pay back everything he stole. But this is the price." His dark eyes narrowed. "You will cut your father completely and permanently out of our lives."

She drew back. "But he's my father. I love him—"

"He lost the right to your loyalty long ago. Do you think I want a con artist, a thief, around my wife…my child…my home?" He looked at her in tightly controlled fury. "No."

"He never meant to hurt anyone," she tried. "He always hoped the stock market would turn and he'd be able to pay everyone back. He just lost his way after my mom died. And he hasn't been well since he got out of prison. If you just knew what he's been through…"

"Excuses on top of excuses! You expect me to feel sympathy?" he said incredulously. "Because he was sick? Because he lost his wife? Because of him, you and I were separated. Because of him, my own father never had the chance to grow old! After he'd worked for him with utter devotion for almost twenty-five years. And that's how your father repaid him!"

"Darius, please."

"You expect me to allow that man to walk you down the aisle? To hold my firstborn child in his arms? No." He set his jaw. "He's a monster. He has no conscience, no soul."

"You don't know him like I do…"

Remembering her weakness where her father was concerned, her senseless loyalty at any cost, Darius abruptly changed tack. "If you truly love him, you will do as I ask. It will benefit him, as well."

"How can you say that?"

"Once I've paid all his debts, he'll never need to be afraid of someone breaking his arm again. He'll be treated better by his probation officers. By potential employers."

"He can't work. No one would hire him. He would starve in the street."

Revulsion churned in Darius's belly, but he forced himself to say, "I will make sure that does not happen. He can remain in your Brooklyn apartment and his rent will be paid. He will always have food and any other necessities he might require. But he must face the consequences of what he's done. He's taken enough from you, Letty. Your future is with me."

Pushing away the breakfast plates, he stood up from the kitchen counter and went to her handbag on the entryway table. Pulling out her phone, he held it out to her.

"Call him," he said quietly. "See what he tells you to do."

Sitting at the counter in her white robe, Letty stared at the phone with big, stricken eyes, as if it were poison. She snatched it up, and with an intake of breath, dialed and held it up to her ear.

"Hi, Dad." She paused, then said unhappily, "Yes. I'm sorry. I don't blame you for worrying. I should have... Ooh? You saw that?" She looked up and said to Darius, "Your announcement about repaying the five billion is already all over the news. Our engagement, too. Dad is thrilled."

"Of course," he said acidly.

"What?" She turned her focus back to her father. "Oh, yes," she whispered, looking up at Darius with troubled eyes. "We're very happy." She bit her lip. "But, Dad, there's this one thing. It's a big thing. A big horrible thing—" her voice broke a little "—and I hardly know how to say it…" She took a deep breath. "I won't be able to see you anymore. Or let you see the baby."

Darius watched her face as she listened to her father's response. Her expression was miserable.

He blocked all mercy from his soul. He was being cruel to be kind. Saving her from her own weak, loving heart.

"No," she whispered into the phone. "I won't abandon you. It's not…"

She paused again, and her expression changed, became numb with grief. Finally, she choked out in a voice almost too soft to hear, "Okay, Dad. All right. I love you, too. So much. Goodbye."

Tears were streaming down her face. Wiping them away, she handed Darius the phone. "He wants to talk to you."

He stared down at the phone in dismay. He hadn't expected that. He picked it up and put it to his ear.

"What do you want?" he said coldly.

"Darius Kyrillos." He recognized Howard Spencer's voice. Though the voice had aged and grown shaky, he could almost hear the older man's smile. "I remember when you were a little boy, just come to Fairholme. You barely spoke English but even then, you were a great kid."

Unwanted memories went through him of when he'd first come to Fairholme with a father who was a stranger to him, a lonely eleven-year-old boy, bereaved by his grandmother's death. He'd felt bewildered by America and homesick for Greece. Back then Howard Spencer had seemed grand and as foreign as a king.

But he'd welcomed the bereft boy warmly. He'd even asked his five-year-old daughter to look after him. In spite of their six-year age difference, Letty, with her caring and friendly heart, had swiftly become his friend, sharing her toys and showing him the fields and beach. While her father had given Darius Christmas presents and told him firmly he could do anything he wanted in life.

In an indirect way, Howard Spencer had even helped start his software company. As a teenager, Darius had been fascinated by computers. He'd taught himself to tinker and code, and soon found himself responsible for every tech device, security feature and bit of wireless connectivity at Fairholme. It was Howard Spencer who'd hired him as the estate's first technical specialist and allowed him to continue to live there. He'd even paid for Darius to study computer science at the local community college...

Darius felt a twist in his gut. Like...guilt? No. He rushed to justify his actions. All right, so Spencer had encouraged him and paid for his schooling. Using stolen money from his Ponzi scheme!

"Yes, a good kid," Howard continued gruffly. "But stubborn, with all that stiff-necked Greek pride. Always had to do everything yourself. Letty was the only one you really let help you with anything. And even then, you always thought you had to be in charge. You never recognized her strength."

"Your point?" Darius said coldly.

He heard the other man take a deep breath.

"Take good care of my daughter," he said quietly. "Both Letty and my grandchild. I know you will. That's the only reason I'm letting them go."

The line abruptly cut off.

"What did he say?" Letty's miserable face came into view.

"He said…" Darius stared down in amazement at the phone in his hand.

He ground his teeth. Damn the old man. Taking the high road. He must be playing the long game. Trusting that Letty would wear him down after their wedding and make him relent. Make him forgive.

But Darius would never forgive. He'd die before he let that man worm his way back into their lives.

"Tell me what he said," Letty pleaded.

He turned to her with an ironic smile. "He gave our marriage his blessing."

Her shoulders slumped.

"That's what he said to me, too," she whispered.

So his theory was correct. Clever bastard, he thought grudgingly. He really knew how to pull his daughter's heartstrings.

But Howard Spencer had finally met someone he couldn't manipulate. The old man would end his days alone, in that tiny run-down apartment, with no one to love him. Just as he deserved.

While they—they would live happily ever after.

Darius looked at Letty tenderly.

After their marriage, after she was legally his forever, she would come to despise her father as Darius did. At the very least, she would forget and let him go.

She would love only Darius, be loyal only to him.

He wouldn't love her back, of course. The childish illusion that love could be anything but pain had been burned out of him permanently. But love was still magic to Letty, and he realized now it was the only way to bind her and make her happy in their marriage. For the sake of their children, he had to make her love him.

This was just the beginning.

"You did the right thing," Darius murmured. Pulling her into his arms, he kissed the top of her head, relishing the feel of her body against his, the crush of her full breasts and her belly rounded with his child. "You'll never regret it."

"I regret it already."

Leaning forward, he kissed the tears off her cheeks. He kissed her forehead, then her eyelids. He felt her shudder and pulled her fully into his arms. He whispered, "Let me comfort you."

He lowered his mouth to hers, gripping her smaller body to his own, and kissed her passionately. A sigh came from her throat as she wrapped her arms around him. He opened the belt of her robe and ran his hands down her naked body. Then with a large sweep of his arm, he knocked all the dishes to the floor with a noisy clatter.

Lifting his future bride up onto the countertop, Darius did what he'd wanted to do for the last hour. He made love to her until she wept. Tears of joy, he told himself. Just tears of joy.

Letty had never been the sort of girl to dream about weddings. At least not since she was eighteen, when her one attempt at elopement had ended so badly.

But she'd vaguely thought, if she ever did get married, she'd have a simple wedding dress, a cake, a bouquet. And her father would give her away.

This wedding had none of that.

Two days after Darius's proposal, they got married in what felt like the worst wedding ever.

Her own fault, Letty thought numbly, as she stood in front of a judge, mumbling vows to honor and cherish. She had no one to blame but herself.

Well, and Darius.

After her phone call with her father, Letty had been too heartsick to care about planning a wedding ceremony. Even Darius ruthlessly taking possession of her body on the kitchen counter hadn't cheered her up. Her heart felt empty and sad.

Darius had tried to tempt her with outrageous ideas for a destination wedding. "If you don't want a big society wedding, there's no reason to wait. The sky's the limit! Do you want a beach wedding in Hawaii? A winter wedding in South America? If you want, I'll rent out the Sydney Opera House. Just say the word!"

She'd looked at him miserably. "What I want is for my father to be there. Without love, what difference does the wedding make?"

The temperature in the room had dropped thirty degrees. "Fine," he said coldly. "If that's how you feel, we might as well just get married at City Hall."

"Fine," she'd said in the same tone.

So they'd gone to the Office of the City Clerk near Chinatown this afternoon, where they'd now been killing time for three hours, surrounded by happy couples all waiting for their turn.

Letty felt exhausted to the bone. She hadn't slept at all the night before. Neither she nor Darius had even bothered to dress up for the ceremony. She wore a simple blouse and maternity pants. Darius wore a dark shirt, dark jeans and a dark glower.

Nor had it helped that the two friends they'd brought to be their witnesses had hated each other on sight. The constant childish bickering between Belle Langtry and Santiago Velazquez, who'd introduced himself as Ángel, had been the final nail in the coffin of Worst Wedding Ever.

It could have been so different, Letty thought sadly. If her father had been there, if she and Darius had been in love, nothing else would have mattered.

But there was no love anywhere on this wedding day.

As she and Darius had sat waiting, listening to their best man and maid of honor squabble, she couldn't stop tears from falling. Darius's glower only made them fall faster.

Their number was the very last to be called in the late afternoon. The four of them had gone up to the desk. As the officiant swiftly and matter-of-factly spoke the words that would bind her to Darius forever, Letty couldn't stop thinking about how she was betraying her father. The man who'd taught her to roller-skate down Fairholme's long marble hallways, who'd taught her chess on rainy days. The man who'd told her again and again how much he loved her.

"I screwed everything up," Howard had told her sadly when he got out of prison. "But I swear I'll make it up to you, Letty. I'll get you back the life you lost…"

He'd never once criticized her for getting pregnant out of wedlock. He'd just been delighted about a future grandchild. Even when she'd phoned him before the wedding, and told him she was marrying Darius, she'd felt his joy. Though it had been abruptly cut off when she'd tearfully told him the rest of the deal.

Then he'd said quietly, "Do it, sweetheart. Marry him. It's what you've always wanted. Knowing you're happy, I'll be at peace."

Now, as she watched Darius speak his marriage vows, Letty's heart twisted. She blinked as she heard the officiant solemnly finish, "…I now pronounce you man and wife."

The whole ceremony had taken three minutes.

She dimly heard Belle clapping and hooting wildly as Darius leaned forward to kiss her. Some instinct made her turn away and offer him only her cheek.

His glower turned radioactive.

After signing the marriage certificate, their small party of four trundled out of the City Clerk's Office to discover the cold gray September skies pouring rain.

"Such a beautiful ceremony. I'm so happy for you," Belle sighed, obviously caught up in some romantic image that had nothing to do with reality. "You make a perfect couple."

"You're living in a fairy tale," Santiago Velazquez muttered. "They can obviously barely stand each other."

Belle whirled on him irritably. "Just once, could you keep your bad attitude to yourself?" Her voice was shrill. "I'm sick of hearing it!"

He shrugged, glancing at Darius. "You got married because she's pregnant, right?"

"Velazquez, don't make me punch you on my wedding day."

"See?" Belle crowed. "Even *Darius* can't stand you."

The Spaniard looked superior. "Just because I'm the only one who is willing to speak the truth…"

"The truth is that marriage is about love and commitment and a whole bunch of sophisticated emotions you obviously can't handle. So keep your opinions to yourself. You might think you're being all deep, but talking like that at a wedding is just plain tacky!"

The Spaniard's eyes narrowed and for a moment Letty was afraid that the constant bickering between them was about to boil over into something truly unpleasant. But to her relief, the man abruptly gave a stiff nod.

"You are right."

Belle stared at him wide-eyed, then tossed her hair, huffing with a flare of her nostrils. "Course I'm right. I'm always right."

Letty exhaled as they seemed to drop the matter.

"Except for when you're wrong," came his sardonic response, "which is every other time but now, since you're obviously living in some ridiculous romantic dream world."

Belle glared at him, then whirled on Letty with a beaming smile. "Are you having a good wedding day, sweetie? Because that's what I care about. Because I'm not rude like some people. We learn manners in Texas."

"I have a ranch in Texas," the Spaniard rejoined. "And I learned an expression that I believe applies to you, Miss Langtry."

"The meek shall inherit the earth?"

He gave her a sensual half smile. "All hat, no cattle."

Belle gave an outraged intake of breath. Then she said sweetly, "That's a lot of big talk for a man with a girl's name."

He looked irritated. "You're saying it wrong. An-hel. And it is a man's name. In every Spanish-speaking country..."

"Aaain-jel, Aaain-jel!" she taunted, using the pronunciation that involved harps and wings. She blinked. "Oh, look, the limo's here."

Letty almost cried in relief.

"Finally," Darius muttered. The limo had barely slowed down at the curb before he opened the back door for his bride. Letty jumped in, eager to escape.

"Where are we going?" Belle said, starting to follow, the Spaniard coming up behind her. Darius blocked them from the limo.

"Thank you so much. Both of you. But I'm afraid Letty and I must leave immediately for Greece."

Belle frowned. "I thought you weren't leaving

until tomorrow. We were going to take you out for dinner…"

"Unfortunately, we must get on the plane immediately. My family is waiting to meet my new bride."

"Oh," Belle said, crestfallen. "In that case… Of course I understand." Leaning into the back of the limo, she hugged Letty. "Have a wonderful honeymoon! You deserve every bit of your happiness!"

Belle was right, Letty reflected numbly as the limo pulled away from her friend still beaming and waving on the sidewalk. She'd get all the happiness she deserved after abandoning her father to marry Darius: none.

Letty stared out at the gray rain. Darius sat beside her silently for the hour and a half it took to drive through the evening rush-hour traffic to the small airport outside the city. As they boarded his private jet, he continued to ignore her.

Fine. Letty didn't care. She felt exhausted and miserable. Walking to the separate bedroom in the back of the jet, she shut the door behind her. Climbing into bed, she pulled the blanket up to her forehead, struggling to hold back tears. She closed her eyes.

And woke up in a different world.

Letty sat up with an intake of breath.

She was no longer on the jet. She found herself in a big, bright bedroom, empty except for a king-size wrought-iron bed.

Brilliant sunlight came through the open windows, leaving warm patterns against the white walls and red tiled floor. She heard laughter outside and conversation in an exotic language and the sweet singing of birds.

She looked down at the soft blanket and cotton sheets. Where was she? And—her lips parted in a gasp. She was wearing only her bra and panties! Someone had undressed her while she was asleep! The thought horrified her.

How had she gotten into this bed?

The flight across the Atlantic had been lonely and dark. She remembered crying herself to sleep on the plane. After her sleepless night before their wedding, she'd slept deeply.

She dimly remembered Darius carrying her, the warmth of his chest, the comforting rumble of his voice.

"So you're awake."

Looking up with an intake of breath, Letty saw her husband now standing in the open doorway, dressed more casually than she'd ever seen him, in a snug black T-shirt and long cargo shorts. Sunlight lit him from behind, leaving his expression in shadow.

"Where are we?"

"The island of Heraklios. My villa."

"I barely remember arriving."

"You were exhausted. Overwhelmed from the happiness of marrying me," he said sardonically.

"What time is it?"

"Here? Almost two in the afternoon." He motioned to a nearby door. "There's an en suite bathroom if you'd like a shower." He indicated a large walk-in closet. "Your clothes have already been unpacked."

"Are you the one who took off my clothes?"

"Just so you'd sleep more comfortably."

She bit her lip as she looked down at the bed. "Um. And did you...did we...uh, share this bed?"

His shoulders tensed. "If you're asking if I took advantage of you in your sleep, the answer is no."

She took a deep breath. "I didn't mean..."

"Get dressed and come out on the terrace when you're ready. My family is here to meet you."

Letty stared at the empty doorway in dismay, then slowly rose out of bed. Her body felt stiff from sleeping so long.

Going into the elegant marble bathroom, she took a hot shower, which refreshed her. Wrapping herself in a towel, she wiped the steam off the mirror. Her face looked pale and sad.

A fine thing, she thought. When she was about to meet his family. They'd take one look at Letty's face and assume, as Santiago Velazquez had, that she and Darius had gotten married only because of her pregnancy. Why else would someone as handsome and powerful as Darius Kyrillos ever choose a penniless, ordinary-looking woman like her?

He was taking a risk even bringing her to meet them. She could embarrass him, treat them disrespectfully. She could even explain how he'd blackmailed her into marriage.

Letty looked at her eyes in the mirror. She didn't want to hurt Darius. She just wanted him to forgive her dad.

Maybe she could start by treating his family with the same respect she wanted for her father.

Letty dressed quickly and carefully, blow-drying her long dark hair and brushing it till it shone. She put on lipstick, and chose a pretty new sundress and sandals from the closet. Her knees shook as she went down the hallway. A maid directed her toward the terrace.

With a deep breath, she went outside into the sunshine.

Bright pink bougainvillea climbed the whitewashed walls of the Greek villa, above a wide terrace overlooking the mountainous slopes of the island jutting out of the Ionian Sea.

Against the blue horizon, she saw the shaded forest green of a distant island. The whole world seemed bright with color: blue and white buildings, sea and sky, pink flowers, brown earth and green olive, fig and pomegranate trees.

She felt the warm sun against her skin, and pleasure seeped through her body. Then she saw the group of people sitting at a long wooden table.

Darius rose abruptly from the table. Silence fell as the others followed his gaze.

Wordlessly, he came over to her. His dark eyes glowed as he lowered his head to kiss her cheek. Turning back to the others, he said in English, "This is Letty. My wife."

An elderly woman got up from the table. Standing on her tiptoes, she squinted, carefully looking Letty over from her blushing face to her pregnant belly. Then she smiled. Reaching up, she patted Letty on the cheek and said something in Greek that she didn't understand.

"My great-aunt says you look happy now," Darius translated. "Like a beautiful bride."

"How sweet... Did she see me before?" Letty asked.

"When I brought you in. She said you looked like death warmed over."

She stared at him in horror, then narrowed her eyes accusingly. "She never said that."

He gave a sudden grin. "She says our island has obviously revived you, all our sun and sea air. Plus, clearly—" he quirked a dark eyebrow "—marriage to me."

The elderly woman said something quickly behind him. He glanced back with an indulgent smile. *"Nai, Theia Ioanna."*

"What did she say?"

Darius turned back to Letty. "She said marriage

to you seems to agree with me, as well." Looking down at her, he hesitated. "Our wedding was…"

"Horrible."

"Not good," he agreed. His dark eyes caressed her face, and he leaned forward to whisper, "But something tells me our honeymoon will make up for it."

Letty felt his breath against her hair, the brush of his lips against her earlobe, and electricity pulsed through her at the untold delights promised by a honeymoon in the Greek villa. In that enormous bed.

She tried not to think about that as he introduced her to the other people around the table, aunts and uncles and innumerable cousins. She smiled shyly, wishing she could speak Greek as one Kyrillos family member after another hugged her, their faces alight with welcome and approval.

One of the younger women grabbed her arm, motioning for her to take the best seat at the table. On learning she was hungry, other relatives dished her out a lunch from the tempting dishes on the table. Tangy olives, salad with cucumbers, tomatoes and feta, vine leaves stuffed with rice, grilled meats on skewers, fresh seafood and finally the lightest, flakiest honey pastries imaginable. After sleeping so long, and having no appetite yesterday, Letty was ravenous and gobbled it all up as fast as she could get it.

The women around her exclaimed approvingly

in Greek. Darius sat beside her, smiling, his dark eyes glowing beneath the warm Greek sun.

"They like how you eat," he told her.

She laughed in spite of herself. In this moment, beneath the pink flowers and warm Greek sun, with the blue sea beyond, she felt suddenly, strangely happy. Finally, she pushed her chair away from the table, shaking her head as his relatives offered yet more plates. "No, thank you." She turned anxiously to Darius. "How do I say that?"

"Óchi, efharisto."

"Óchi, efharisto," she repeated to them warmly.

One by one, his family members hugged her, speaking rapidly, patting her belly, then hugging Darius before they hurried into the villa.

"Your family is wonderful."

"Thank you." He lifted a dark eyebrow. "By the way, some of them speak English quite well. They're just hoping if you don't realize that, you'll be inspired to learn Greek."

She laughed, then looked around the terrace at the flowers and sea view. "I'm feeling very inspired, believe me."

"They already love you. Because you're my wife." He put his arm along the back of her chair. "Not only that, you're the first woman I've ever brought home to meet them."

Her eyes went wide. "Really?"

He grinned, shaking his head. "For years, they read about my scandalous love life and despaired of me ever settling down with a nice girl." He sipped strong black coffee from a tiny cup. "Great-aunt Ioanna is delirious with joy to see me not only sensibly married, but also expecting a child. And she remembers you."

Letty's smile fell. "She does?"

"Yes."

"Does she blame me for—?"

"No," he cut her off. "She remembers you only as the girl that I loved and lost long ago. In her mind, that means our marriage is fate. *Moíra.* She believes our love was meant to stand the test of time."

Letty blinked fast. *Our love was meant to stand the test of time.*

Leaning forward, he took her hand. "You are part of the family. You are a Kyrillos now."

It was true, she realized. She had a new last name. When she updated her passport, she'd no longer be Letitia Spencer, the daughter of the famous white-collar criminal, but Letitia Kyrillos, the wife of a self-made billionaire. Just by marrying, she'd become an entirely different person. What a strange thought.

But maybe this new woman, Letitia Kyrillos, would know how to be happy. Maybe their marriage, which had been so bleak at the start, could someday be full of joy, as her own parents' marriage had been.

She just had to change Darius's mind about her father. It wouldn't be hard.

Like making it snow in July.

One of Darius's female cousins came back out of the villa and pulled on his arm, talking rapidly in Greek, even as she smiled apologetically at Letty.

"They need to move the big table," he explained. "To get the terrace ready for the party tonight."

"What party?"

"They wouldn't let us come all this way without making a big fuss." He grinned. "There's a party tonight to welcome you as my bride. Only family and friends from the village have been invited..."

"Good," she said, relieved.

"Which, naturally, means the entire island will be here, and a few people from neighboring islands, as well."

Her heart sank to her sandals at the thought of all those people judging her, possibly finding her unworthy of being Darius's bride. She whispered, "What if they don't like me?"

Reaching out, Darius lifted her chin. "Of course they will," he said softly. "They will because I do."

As the hot Greek sun caressed her skin in the flower-dappled terrace, the dark promise in his gaze made her shiver.

As his relatives bustled back out on the terrace, with maids following them, they started clearing dishes, wiping the table and sweeping the terrace.

Letty looked around anxiously. "Ask them how I can help."

He snorted. "If you think they'll allow either of us to lift a finger, you're out of your mind."

"We can't just sit here, while they do all the work!"

"Watch this." Pushing his chair back, Darius rose from the table and said casually in English, "Hey, Athina, hand me that broom."

"Forget it, Darius," his cousin replied indignantly in the same language, yanking the broom out of his reach. "You sent my sons to college!"

"You gave me a job when I needed work," a man added in heavily accented English, as he lifted fairy lights to dangle from the terrace's leafy trellis. "We're doing this. Don't think you're getting out of it!"

They all gave a low buzz of agreement.

Looking at Letty, Darius shrugged. She sighed, seeing she was outmatched. His great-aunt was now, in fact, shooing them away with a stream of steady Greek, a mischievous smile on her kindly, wizened face.

Letty drew closer to him. "So what should we do with ourselves?"

Darius's eyes darkened as he said huskily, "We *are* on our honeymoon…"

She shivered at his closeness and at the tempting thought of going back to the bedroom. But she was distracted by the sweep of the brooms and the loud cries of the relatives and house staff bustling back and forth across the villa as they cleaned and set up for the party, all the while watching Darius and Letty out of the corners of their eyes with frank interest and indulgent smiles.

"I couldn't," Letty whispered, blushing beneath all the stares. "If we stay, I'll feel like we should help cook and clean."

"Then let's not stay." He took her hand. "Let me show you the island."

He drew her out of the enormous, luxurious villa, past the gate and out onto unpaved road. Looking around, she saw the rural rolling hills were covered with olive and pomegranate trees, dotted with small whitewashed houses beneath the sun. But there was one thing she didn't see.

"Where are all the cars? The paved roads?"

"We don't have cars. Heraklios is too small and mountainous, and there are only a few hundred residents. There are a few cobblestoned streets by the waterfront, but they're too winding and tight for any car."

"So how do you get around?"

"Donkey."

She almost tripped on her own feet. She looked at him incredulously. "You're joking."

He grinned. "I managed to put in a helicopter pad, and also a landing strip, at great expense, and it isn't even usable if the wind is too strong. Here we transport most things by sea." As they walked closer to an actual village clinging to a rocky cliff, he pointed to a small building on a hill. "That was my school."

"It looks like one room."

"It is. After primary school, kids have to take a ferry to a bigger school the next island over." As they continued walking, he pointed to a small *taverna*. "That's where I tasted my first sip of *retsina*." His nose wrinkled. "I spit it out. I still don't like it."

"And you call yourself a Greek," she teased. His eyebrow quirked at her challenge.

"I'd take you in and let you taste it, except—" he looked more closely at the closed door "—it looks like old Mr. Papadakis is already up at the villa. Probably setting up drinks."

"The whole town's closing—just for our wedding reception?"

"It's a small island. I don't think you realize how much pull I have around here."

Letty slowed when she saw a ruined, lonely-looking villa at the top of the hill, above the village. "What's that?"

His lips tightened, curled up at the edges. "That was my mother's house."

"Oh," she breathed. She knew his mother had abandoned him at birth. He'd never talked much about her, not even when they were young. "No one lives there anymore?"

"My mother left the island right after I was born,

her parents soon after. It seems they couldn't stand the shame of my existence," he added lightly.

She flinched, her heart aching. "Oh, Darius."

"My mother moved to Paris. She died in a car crash when I was around four." He shrugged. "I heard her parents died a few years ago. I can't remember where or how."

"I'm so sorry."

"Why? I didn't love them. I don't mourn them."

"But your mother. Your grandparents…"

"Calla Halkias died in a limousine, married to an aristocrat." His voice was cold as he looked back to the ghostly ruin on the hill. "Just as I'm sure she would have wanted. The prestigious life her parents expected for her."

A lump rose in her throat as she thought of Darius as a child on this island, looking up at the imposing villa of the people who'd tossed him out like garbage. She didn't know what to say, so she held his hand tightly. "Did you ever forgive them?"

"For what?"

"They were your family, and they abandoned you."

His lips pressed down. "My mother gave birth to me. I'm glad about that. But I wouldn't call them *family*. From everything I've heard, they were a total disaster. Like…" He hesitated. But she knew.

"Like my family?" she said quietly.

He paused. "Your mother was a great lady. She was always kind. To everyone."

"Yes," she said over the lump in her throat.

"My *yiayiá* raised me. Our house didn't have electricity or plumbing, but I always knew she loved me. When I finally made my fortune, I had the old shack razed and built a villa in its place. The biggest villa this island has ever seen." Looking up at the ruin, he gave a grim smile. "When I was young, the Halkias family was the most powerful here. Now I am."

She noticed he'd never said if he forgave them. She bit her lip. "But, Darius…"

"It's in the past. I want to live in the present. And shape the future." Taking both her hands in his own, Darius looked down at her seriously on the dusty road beneath the hot Greek sun. "Promise me, Letty. You'll always do what's best for our family."

"I promise," she said, meaning it with all her heart.

Lowering his head, he whispered, "And I promise the same."

He softly kissed her, as if sealing the vow. Drawing back, he searched her gaze. Then he pulled her back into his arms and kissed her in another way entirely.

Feeling the heat of his lips against hers, the rough scrape of the bristles on his chin, she clung to him, lost in her own desire. He was her husband now. *Her husband.*

He finally pulled away. "Come with me."

He led her to the end of the dusty road, through the winding cobblestones of the small village of whitewashed houses. On the other side, they went through a scrub brush thicket of olive trees. She held his hand tightly as the branches scraped her arms, and they went down a sharp rocky hill. Then suddenly, they were in a hidden cove on a deserted white sand beach.

Letty's eyes went wide in amazement. The popular beaches of the Hamptons and even around Fairholme would have been packed on a gloriously warm September day. But this beach was empty. "Where is everyone?"

"I told you. They're at the villa, getting ready for the party."

"But—" she gestured helplessly "—there must be tourists, at least?"

He shook his head. "We don't have a hotel. The tourists are at the resorts up in Corfu. So we all know each other here. Everyone is a friend or relative, or at least a friend of a relative. It's a community. One big family."

No wonder this island felt like a world out of time. She felt her heart twist. Turning away, she looked around at the hidden cove with the white sand beach against the blue Ionian Sea and tried to smile. "It's wonderful."

"You're missing Fairholme," he said quietly.

She looked down at the white sand. "It's been

ten years. It's stupid. Any psychiatrist would tell me it's time to let it go."

"I miss it, too." He grinned. "Do you remember the beach at Fairholme? Nothing but rocks."

"Yes, and the flower meadow where you taught me to dance."

"What about the pond where I tried to catch frogs and you always wanted to give them names and take them home—?"

Suddenly their words were tumbling over each other.

"The brilliant color of the trees in autumn—"

"Roller-skating down the hallways—"

"The secret passageway behind the library where you'd always hide when you were upset—"

"Your mother's rose garden," Darius said with a sudden laugh, "where she caught me that time I tried a cigarette. My first and last time—"

"And how Mrs. Pollifax scolded us whenever we tracked mud into her freshly cleaned kitchen." Letty grinned. "But she always gave us milk and cookies after we'd made it right. Though it took a while. You weren't very good at mopping."

"We always turned it into a game."

The two of them smiled at each other on the deserted beach.

Letty's smile slipped away. "But we'll never see Fairholme again."

Darius stared at her for a long moment, then

abruptly started taking off his shoes. "The sea should be warm."

She lifted her eyebrows. "What are you doing?"

"I'm getting in." He leaned over to unbuckle her sandals. "And you're coming with me."

Barefoot, they went splashing out into the sea. Letty delighted in the feel of the water caressing her feet, then her calves and finally knees. She was tempted to go deeper into the water, to float her pregnant body in the seductive waves that would make her feel light as air. She took a few more steps, until the sea lapped the hem of her white sundress.

Splashing behind her, Darius suddenly pulled her into his arms.

As the waves swirled around them, he kissed her, and there was no one to see but the birds soaring across the sky. For hours, or maybe just minutes, they kissed in the hidden cove, between the bright blue sea and sky, beneath the hot Greek sun. He ran his hands over her bare shoulders, over her thin cotton sundress, as the salty sea spray clung to their skin and hair.

Waves swirled around them, sucking the sand beneath their toes, as the tide started to come in. The waves crashed higher, moving up against their thighs.

Finally pulling away, Darius looked down at her intently. She felt his dark gaze sear her body. Sear her heart.

"Letty, the house we grew up in might be gone," he whispered. "But we still have each other."

The lowering afternoon sun shone around the edges of his dark hair, making Darius shimmer like the dream he was to her.

And it was then Letty knew the worst had happened. The doom and disaster. And it had happened more swiftly than she'd ever expected.

She loved him.

All of him.

The man he'd been.

The man he was.

The man he could be.

Since the February night they'd conceived their child, Letty had tried to convince herself that he'd changed irrevocably. That she hated him. That he'd lost her love forever.

It had all been a lie.

Even in her greatest pain, she'd never stopped loving him. How could she? He was the love of her life.

Glancing back at the lowering sun, Darius sighed. "Can't be late for our own party. We'd better get back to the villa." He glanced down at his shorts, now splattered with sand and seawater. "We might have to clean up a little."

"Yes," she said in a small voice.

"We'll finish this later," he said huskily, kissing her bare shoulder. He whispered, "I can hardly wait to make love to you, Mrs. Kyrillos."

As they splashed their way to the beach, and made their way up the shore, Letty stumbled.

He caught her, then frowned, looking at her closely. "Did you hurt yourself?"

"No," she said, hiding the ache in her throat, struggling to hold back tears. It wasn't totally a lie. She wasn't hurt.

But she knew she soon would be.

One day married, and her heart was already lost.

CHAPTER NINE

DARIUS NEARLY GASPED when he first saw Letty at the party that night. When she came out onto the terrace, she looked so beautiful she seemed to float through the twilight.

She wore a simple white maxi dress, which fit perfectly over her full breasts and baby bump. The soft fabric showed off the creamy blush of her skin and bright hazel of her eyes. Bright pink flowers hung in her long dark hair.

As the red sun was setting into the sea below the cliffs, three hundred people on the terrace burst into spontaneous applause amid a cacophony of approving Greek.

Darius's heart was in his throat as he looked at her. He was dazzled. He thought she'd put Aphrodite, freshly risen from the sea, completely to shame.

And the fact that he'd even have such a ridiculously poetic thought stunned him.

As she came closer, he cleared his throat awkwardly. "You look nice."

"Thank you," she said, smiling shyly.

He did not touch her. He was almost afraid to. She was simply too desirable, and after their hours of kissing on the beach, he did not know how much more temptation his self-control could take. They'd been married for over twenty-four hours, but had not yet made love.

The party was torture. It lasted for hours, testing his resolve. If it had been any other situation, he would have told everyone to go to hell and taken his bride straight to bed.

But this was his family. His village. He couldn't be rude to them or reject the warm welcome they gave his bride.

His whole body ached to possess her. He could think of nothing else. It was causing him physical pain. He was just glad he was wearing a long, loosely tailored jacket and loose trousers so the whole village could not discuss with amused approval his obvious desire for his bride.

The party was over the top, as only village affairs could be, with music, drinking and dancing. A feast had been lovingly prepared by his family and all the rest of the village. So many people rushed to Letty and started talking excitedly in Greek that she'd announced she planned to start taking Greek lessons as soon as possible. Some of his cousins immediately started cheering, and when Darius translated her words for his elderly great-aunt, Theia Ioanna actually stood on tiptoe to kiss Letty on both cheeks. His family loved her.

Of course they did. Letty Kyrillos was the perfect bride. She would be the perfect wife and mother. Now he'd gotten her away from her father, there would be no bad influences in her life.

Darius would be the only one to claim her loyalty. And the expression in Letty's eyes as she looked at him now—a mix of longing, hero worship and fear—did strange things to his insides. It made him feel oddly vulnerable, reminding him of the insecure, lovesick youth he'd once been for her.

No. He just desired her, he told himself firmly. He was appreciative that she was comporting herself as a proper Greek wife, with kindness and respect to his family. And he hoped—expected—that she would soon love him. It would make all their lives easier.

Darius did not intend to love her in return. He would never leave himself that vulnerable again. As the protector of their family, as a husband, as a father, as a man, it was his duty to be strong.

Letty's heart was her weakness. It would not be his.

His great-aunt went to bed at midnight, and the rest of the older generation soon after, but with the ouzo flowing and loud music and enthusiastic dancing, his cousins and many of the younger villagers remained well into the wee hours. It wasn't until the ouzo was gone and the musicians were falling asleep over their instruments that the last guests finally took the hint and departed, after many congratulations and kisses for the newly married couple.

Darius and Letty were finally alone on the terrace, surrounded by streamers and empty champagne glasses.

She looked at him, her eyes huge in the moonlight, the pink flowers wilting in her dark lustrous hair.

Without a word, he took her hand.

Leading her to their bedroom suite at the farthest end of the south wing, he closed the door behind them and opened the windows and sliding glass door to the balcony. The wind blew from the sea, twisting the translucent white curtains, illuminated by moonlight.

Turning back to her, he lifted her long dark hair from the nape of her neck and slowly unzipped her dress. In the hush of the night, it felt like an act that was almost holy.

Her dress dropped to the floor. She turned to him, her eyes luminous in the silvery light. Reaching up, she pulled off his jacket. She unbuttoned his shirt. He felt the soft brush of her hands against his chest and caught them in his own. She looked up at him questioningly.

A strange feeling was building in his heart. *Desire*, he reminded himself fiercely. *I desire her.* He kissed her hands—first one, then the other.

The wind blew against her hair, causing pink flower petals to float softly to the floor like a benediction. Without a word, he pulled her to the enormous bed.

This time, as they made love, there were no words beyond the language of touch. There was only pleasure and delight.

He'd thought he'd known ecstasy the night they'd made love over and over in his Manhattan penthouse.

But this was something else. It felt different.

Why? Because they were married now, and she was permanently his? Because she knew him better than anyone on earth? Because she'd truly joined his family?

Whatever the reason, as he made love to her on this, their first true wedding night, it felt sacred.

It felt like…

Happiness.

After they'd both joined and shattered like a supernova in each other's arms, Darius held her as she slept. As he stared at the ceiling, her words on the beach floated back into his mind.

We'll never see Fairholme again.

Her voice had been quietly despairing. As if she'd accepted bleak loss as her due.

Darius scowled. He didn't accept that.

He suddenly wanted to give Letty back everything she'd lost. And more.

Careful not to wake her, he rose from the bed in the gray light of dawn. Going out onto the balcony, with its view of the wild gray sea, he made a quiet phone call to his long-suffering executive assistant in New York. Mildred Harrison had worked for him for seven years, so she didn't even sound surprised that he'd be rude enough to call her so late.

"Pity you left New York right when you're the city's hero," she said drily. "Your picture is on the cover of the *Daily Post*. Apparently you're some kind of Robin Hood figure now, robbing from your own fortune to pay back Howard Spencer's victims."

"Glad I'm not there, then. We'll be back in two weeks, by which time I expect the papers will all be insulting me again. Anything else?"

"That Brooklyn apartment building has been purchased as you requested. Your father-in-law—"

"Never call him that again," Darius said tersely.

She cleared her throat. "Um, Mr. Spencer has been advised that he will be allowed to remain in the apartment for as long as he wishes, free of charge."

"Good," he said, already bored with the subject.

She paused. "There's something else you should know."

"Well?"

"The investigator following him says Spencer has been visiting an oncologist. Apparently he's sick. Maybe dying."

Darius's eyes widened. Then he gave a snort. "It's a trick."

"Mr. Green didn't think so. He managed to get his hands on the medical records. It seems legit."

"Spencer must have paid the doctor off."

"Maybe." Mildred sounded doubtful. "But if it were my father, I'd still want to know."

Yes, Darius thought. He looked back at the shadowy form of Letty sleeping in his bed. She would want to know. But there was no way he was telling her. Not when the old man was probably just trying once again to cause trouble between them.

At worst, Spencer probably had a cold and thought he could use it to get out of his well-deserved punishment. Darius was not going to let it happen.

"I won't have my wife bothered," he said shortly. "Spencer must have known he was being followed."

"As you say, Mr. Kyrillos."

He set his jaw. "I called you for another reason. I want to buy my wife a wedding gift."

"Beyond the billions you're already putting in trust for her father's victims? We've had a whole team of accountants coming through here, by the way, working with the Feds to determine accurate payments, including those for third-party clients. We're not really staffed for this…"

"You'll sort it out. And at the end, I'll send you and your husband to Miami for a week of well-deserved rest."

"Rome," she said firmly. "For three."

He grinned. Mildred knew what she was worth. He respected that.

"Three," he agreed. "But I need you to do something first. I want to buy a home."

"Your penthouse is too small?"

"I have a special place in mind. Find out what it would cost."

He explained, and she gave a low whistle. "All right, boss. I'll call you soon as I know. What's your ceiling?"

"Whatever it takes."

After he hung up the phone, Darius went back to the king-size bed he shared with his pregnant bride. Joining her under the blankets, he wrapped his arm around her as she slept. He heard the birds singing as, outside the window, the sun started to rise.

Holding Letty in his arms, he suddenly saw the reward for everything he'd done right in his life. He had Letty. He'd have the rest. Home. Children. Joy. All the things he'd stopped dreaming about long ago. He would have it all.

And nothing, especially not her criminal of a father, would come between them.

As their private jet began its descent through the clouds toward New York City, Letty felt a mixed sense of relief and regret.

She was glad to be returning closer to her father. Darius had assured her that Howard was fine and living rent-free in their old apartment with a stipend to supply his needs. "Your father is spending his days playing chess with friends down at the park," he'd told her irritably. She could only assume Darius had someone watching him, but she didn't even mind because she was glad to know he was all right. It felt so wrong never to see him, never to call him.

But at least now she'd know her dad was only a quick drive away, if needed. And soon she hoped he'd be back in their lives for good.

The heart attack that had caused the death of Darius's father was a tragic accident. But surely he couldn't hate her dad forever? She loved Darius too much to believe that. Soon they would all be a family again.

And family was all Letty cared about. As she'd promised her husband in Greece, she would always put her family above everything else.

She already felt wistful for the tiny Greek island where she'd been immediately accepted into Darius's extended family. Their honeymoon had been the happiest two weeks of her life. She'd loved everything about Heraklios. The village. The beach. The vivid colors and bright sun. The villa. The people. Her eyes met Darius's across the airplane cabin.

The man.

He was sitting in a white swivel chair and had spent much of the flight typing on his laptop, with some idea he'd had for a new business venture. But as his gaze caught hers, she felt every bit of his attention. She always felt it to her toes when he looked at her.

Lifting a dark eyebrow, he teased, "We could still turn the plane around."

"I loved our visit," she said wistfully, then glanced out the window. "But it'll be nice to be back home." She paused, biting her lip. She knew she shouldn't ask, but she couldn't help it. "Now we're back in the city, maybe you could talk to my dad. Then you'd see his side…"

"Forget it," he said flatly.

"He never meant to hurt anyone, he—"

Darius closed his laptop with a thud. "Stop."

"Forgiveness frees the soul. You never know—" her voice sounded desperate even to her own ears "—*you* might have to ask someone for forgiveness one day!"

He snorted. "I don't intend to commit any crimes, so I think I'm safe."

"Darius—"

"No."

Disappointment filled her heart. Clenching her hands, she told herself she'd just have to be patient. She forced herself to take a deep breath and change the subject. "I loved spending time with your family. Maybe your great-aunt could come visit us in New York."

His expression relaxed and he smiled. "Theia Ioanna hates planes. She thinks of them as new-fangled machines, a dangerous fad. She's waiting for everyone to come to their senses. But after our baby's born we could go back to Heraklios."

"I'd like that." Outside the window, the plane was descending through clouds that looked like white cotton candy. "In the meantime, I'm going to start learning Greek." She looked at him coyly beneath her lashes. "You'd like to teach me your native tongue, wouldn't you?"

His eyes darkened with interest. He started to rise from his seat, but as the plane broke beneath the clouds, the pilot announced over the intercom that they should buckle their seat belts for landing. Letty smiled.

Then she looked through the porthole window. "That's not Teterboro."

Now he was the one to smile. "No."

Staring down, she suddenly recognized the airport. Long ago, her family had landed here every time they went on a trip. She looked up with a frown. "Long Island? Is there a problem?"

"Wait and see."

After the plane landed at the small airport, the two of them came down the steps. A town car waited on the tarmac, and his driver and bodyguard swiftly loaded their suitcases from the plane.

"But why are we here?" she asked Darius helplessly in the backseat of the car a few minutes later as it pulled away from the airport.

"You'll see."

"You're really vexing."

His dark eyebrows lifted. "Vexing?" he teased, then moved closer as he whispered, "Is that what I am?"

Then he kissed her senseless in the backseat, until she was forced to agree rather unsteadily that he did have one or two good qualities, as well.

But she tensed when the limo turned onto the coastal road that she'd once known very, very well. Her suspicions were confirmed as they drove down the same country lane that she knew led to the massive 1920s beachfront estate that had once been her home. She turned on Darius angrily.

"Why would you bring us here?" she choked out. "Just to torture me? You can't see the house from the road." She felt a sudden ache in her throat as she looked out toward the gray-blue bay that led to the Atlantic. "The gate is guarded. That tech billionaire is serious about privacy. So if you're hoping to get a peek of the house, it won't happen."

"You tried?"

"A month after it was sold at auction. As I told you, I just wanted a picture of my great-grandmother's fresco. His guard did everything but set the dogs on me."

"That won't be a problem today."

Letty pointed at the road ahead. "See? I told you—"

Then her eyes went wide.

The gate was wide open. Their limo drove right past the empty guardhouse, up the wide driveway to the glorious windswept oceanfront manor that had been built by Letty's great-great-grandfather, a steel baron named Edwin Langford.

Fairholme.

Letty's breath caught in her throat as she leaned out the car window, and her eyes were dazzled as she saw, for the first time in ten years, her beloved home.

Tears swelled in her eyes as she looked up at the gray stone mansion with its turrets and leaded glass windows soaring against the sky. Looking back at her husband, she breathed, "What have you done?"

He was smiling. "I've given you what you want most."

The limo had barely stopped before she flung open her car door and raced eagerly into the house. Pushing aside the stately front door—unlocked!—she hurled herself into the foyer where she'd played as a child.

"Dad?" she cried out. "Dad, where are you?"

Letty ran from room to room, calling his name, overwhelmed with happiness that somehow, while pretending he was never going to forgive her father, Darius had seen the desperate desire of her heart.

I've given you what you want most.

"Dad!" she cried, moving from one elegant, empty room to the next. Memories followed her with every step.

There she had played pirates with her father.

There she had slipped down the marble floor in socks as the two of them competed to see who could slide farthest and make her mother laugh loudest.

There she'd played with the gardener's kittens.

There she'd played hide-and-seek with Darius when they were kids…

There—every Saturday in summer—she'd tucked roses into the priceless Ming dynasty vase to make her mother smile.

But where was her dad? Where?

As Letty finished going through the main entrance rooms, she ran up the sweeping staircase toward the second floor. She stopped halfway up the stairs, realizing she was hearing only the echo of her own voice.

Her dad wasn't there.

Letty's shoulders sagged with savage disappointment. Turning back down the stairs, she saw Darius standing in the front doorway, watching her. The happy, smug expression had disappeared from his handsome face.

He said tightly, "Why do you think I would invite your father here?"

"You said—you said," she faltered, biting her lip, "you were giving me what I wanted most."

"This house." His expression now could only be described as grimly outraged. "Your childhood home. I arranged to buy it for you. It wasn't easy. I had to pay the man a fortune to leave before we arrived. But I wanted you to have all your dreams. Everything you'd lost."

Everything she'd lost...

Gripping the banister for support, Letty sagged to sit on a stair. Heartbreaking grief was thundering through her, worse than if she'd never gotten her hopes up at all.

She struggled to hide it. She knew she was being churlish. Her mother would be ashamed of her. Here Darius had given her the stars and she was crying for the sun.

She should be overjoyed.

Fairholme.

Letty took a deep breath, looking up at the high painted ceilings, at the oak-paneled walls. *Home.* She was really here. Darius had given her back the home that had raised generations of Langfords, her mother's family.

What an amazing gift.

Wiping her eyes, Letty looked at Darius and tried to smile.

His handsome face was mutinous.

She couldn't blame him. He'd gone to a lot of trouble and expense to give her this incredible surprise, and she'd been completely ungrateful.

Rising unsteadily to her feet, she walked down the stairs to the foyer where he stood with a scowl, his arms folded.

"Thank you," she whispered. "I love your wonderful gift."

He looked distinctly grumpy. "It didn't look like it."

Feeling ashamed at her bad manners, she wrapped her arms around his neck and kissed him.

"I love it," she said softly. "It's a miracle to be here."

Looking mollified, he accepted her embrace. "I've also hired Mrs. Pollifax to come back as our housekeeper."

"You have!"

He smiled, clearly pleased by her reaction. "Along with as many of the original staff who were available. Giving them a big raise, naturally. I've also established a bank account in your name."

"Whatever for?"

Darius gave her a sudden grin. "You obviously haven't seen the stripper pole the last owner put up in the library. I knew you'd want to oversee the remodeling personally. Perhaps the fresco can be repaired? I've instructed the bank to give you unlimited funds. Use the money however you please."

"For the house?"

"Yes."

"The baby?"

"Of course. And you, Letty. Anything you want, jewelry, cars, furniture. You don't have to ask me. Buy anything you desire."

Biting her lip, she blurted out, "Could I send some money to my father?"

She knew immediately it was a mistake.

His expression turned icy. "I weary of your constantly bringing up this topic. We have an agreement."

"I know, but—"

"Your father already has far more than he deserves."

"If I could only just see him, so I could know he's all right…"

"He's fine."

Letty searched his gaze, hoping for reassurance. "He's fine? You know for sure?"

He paused. Then he finally said, "Yes."

He wouldn't meet her eyes.

"I miss him," she whispered. She took a deep breath, reminding herself of everything she had to be grateful for. Taking Darius's hand, she pressed it to her cheek and looked up at him with gratitude. "But what you've done for me today, buying Fairholme back…I'll never forget."

For a long moment, the two of them stood together in the foyer, with sunlight pouring in through the open door. She breathed in scents she'd craved so long, the tangy salt of the ocean, the honeyed sweetness of her mother's rose garden. The salt and sweetness of a lifetime of memories.

"Thank you," she whispered. "For bringing me home."

He cupped her cheek. "You're worth it, Letty," he said huskily. "For you, I would pay any price."

Lowering his head, he kissed her, claiming her

lips as he'd already claimed her body and soul. Words lifted unbidden to her throat. Words she hadn't tried to say since that horrible night in February. Words straight from her heart.

"I love you, Darius," she said softly.

He gave her an oddly shy smile. "You do?"

Smiling back through her tears, she nodded. Her blood was rushing through her ears, pounding through her veins, as she waited for what he'd say next.

Without a word, he kissed her.

As she stood in the Fairholme foyer, her heavily pregnant belly pressed between them as her husband kissed her so tenderly, miracles seemed to be spinning around her like a whirlwind.

They were married now. Expecting a baby. He'd paid off her father's debts. He'd just brought her home. She loved him.

And someday, he would love her.

Letty was suddenly sure. They'd already had so many miracles. Why not more?

Darius would soon forgive her father and let him back into their family. He was too good a man not to forgive, especially when it meant so much to her. It was the only thing he hadn't given her. That, and those three little words.

It was the same thing, she realized. When he forgave her father, that was how she would know that he truly loved her.

When he finally pulled away from their embrace, she looked up, still a little dazzled. "Is there really a stripper pole in the library?"

Darius gave a low laugh. "Come with me."

Taking her hand, he drew her down the long marble hallway to the oak-paneled library. When she saw the gleaming stripper pole set in the brand-new white shag carpeting, she burst into horrified snorts of laughter.

"I told you," he said.

"I'll get it removed. Don't worry. I'll make this house just like it was," Letty said. "Just like we remember."

"All those memories." He pulled her against his chest, his dark eyes intense as he whispered huskily, "But as I remember, there's one thing we've never done in this house."

And as her husband pulled her against him in a hot, fierce embrace, Letty knew all her deepest dreams were about to come true.

CHAPTER TEN

HOME. LETTY LOOKED around with satisfaction. Was there any sweeter word?

The remodel was finished just in time, too. The former owner's monstrous decor had been removed—the shag carpeting, the stripper pole, the "ironic" brass fixtures and all the rest of it—and everything at Fairholme had been returned to its former glory.

The sitting room felt cozy, especially compared to the cold November weather outside. A fire crackled in the fireplace. Polished oak floors gleamed beneath priceless Turkish rugs. The sofas and chairs were plush and comfortable, the lamps sturdy and practical. Family photos now decorated the walls.

Letty snuggled back against the sofa. Her husband was sitting at the other end, tapping away on his laptop, but periodically he would rub her feet, so she made sure they were strategically available. Earlier, they'd had a delicious hearty meal of lamb stew and homemade bread, her favorite meal from childhood, prepared by Mrs. Pollifax.

The housekeeper had just left, saying that she needed to go visit a friend at a Brooklyn hospital.

She'd had a strange expression when she said it, causing Letty to reply with a sympathetic murmur, "Please take all the time you need for your friend."

"I just might," the housekeeper had replied tartly, "since his own family can't be bothered to go see him."

"Poor man," Letty had sighed, feeling sorry for him. She couldn't imagine what kind of family wouldn't visit a sick man in the hospital.

That reminded her of how much she missed her father after more than two months of not seeing him or talking to him. Darius still refused to forgive him. But surely, after their baby was born, his heart would be so full, he would have a new capacity to forgive? To love.

Letty looked at her husband hopefully. With the departure of Mrs. Pollifax, and the rest of the staff in their outlying cottages on the estate, the two of them were now completely alone in the house. The room felt snug and warm with her afghan blanket, the crackling fire and Darius's closeness as outside the cold November wind blew, rattling the leaded glass windows.

She was getting close to her due date, and happier than she'd ever imagined.

The nursery was ready. She'd been overjoyed to discover that her great-grandmother's precious fresco hadn't been completely destroyed. A well-known art restorer had managed to bring a good portion of it back to life. The ducks and geese were far fewer in number, and the Bavarian village mostly gone, but the little goose girl no longer looked so sad. It was a joy to see it again, and though Darius pretended to mock it and roll his eyes as he called it "art," she knew he was happy for her.

The nursery was the most beautiful room in the house, in Letty's opinion, the place where she'd slept as a baby, as had her mother and her grandfather before. It was now freshly painted and decorated, with a crib and rocking chair and brand-new toys. All they needed was the baby.

"Soon," she whispered aloud, rubbing her enormous belly. "Very soon."

"Talking to the baby again?" Darius teased.

Holding up a tattered copy of a beloved children's book, she responded archly, "I'm just going to read him this story."

His dark eyebrows lifted. "Again?"

"The pregnancy book said…"

"Oh, have you read a pregnancy book?"

Letty's lips quirked. Her constant consultation of pregnancy books and blogs was a running joke between them. But as a first-time mother and an only child, she had little experience with children and was anxious to do it right.

"It's been scientifically proven," she informed him now, "that a baby can hear, and therefore obviously listen to stories, from the womb."

He rolled his eyes, then put his large hand tenderly on her belly. "Don't worry, kid," he said in a whisper. "I have something to read you that I know you'll find way more interesting than the bunny story."

"Oh, you do, do you?" she said, amused.

"Absolutely." Turning back to his laptop, he clicked a few buttons and then started reading aloud, with mock seriousness, the latest business news from overseas.

Now she was the one to roll her eyes. But she found Darius's low, deep voice soothing, even when he was describing boring tech developments. Sipping orange spice herbal tea, she nibbled on the sugar cookies she'd made earlier that afternoon. She'd been eating so much lately she felt nearly as big as a house herself.

But Darius didn't seem to mind. Her cheeks grew hot as she recalled how he'd made love to her all over the house. Even the bathrooms—those with showers, at least. Almost forty rooms.

"We have to make this house ours," he'd growled, and she'd loved it.

Now as she felt his gentle hand resting on her belly, she grew drowsy listening to his low voice reading news stories to their baby and punctuating them with exclamations when he felt the baby kick.

"Letty," Darius said in a low voice, "are you awake?"

"Barely." She yawned. "I was just going to head up to bed. Why?"

He was quiet for a long moment, then said quietly, "Never mind. It'll wait. Good night, *agape mou.*"

The next morning, she kissed Darius goodbye as he left for lower Manhattan, as was his usual schedule Monday through Thursday. He'd set up an office for a new business he was excited about, to create software that would teach math and coding skills. Each day, Darius hired more employees, paying for their salaries out of his own pocket. There hadn't been any profits. "And there might never be any," he'd confessed sheepishly. But he wanted to make a difference in the world.

She'd never been so proud of him. He had a new spark in his eyes as he left Fairholme for his ninety-minute commute to the office.

Letty went up to the nursery, her favorite room, to fold all the cute tiny baby clothes one more time and make sure everything was ready. She'd had a dull ache in her lower back all morning. She went down to the kitchen, intending to ask Mrs. Pollifax if she knew of any natural remedy for back pain.

Instead she found the housekeeper crying.

"What's wrong?" Letty cried, going up to her in the enormous, gleaming kitchen. "What's happened?"

"My friend." The woman wiped her eyes with the edge of her apron. "He's dying."

"I'm so sorry," Letty whispered.

Mrs. Pollifax's eyes looked at her accusingly. "You should be. Since it's your own father."

Letty stared at her in shock. For a long minute, she couldn't even make sense of the words.

"I'm sorry—I can't be silent any longer," the housekeeper said. "Whatever caused you to be estranged from him, you're wrong to let him die alone. You'll regret it the rest of your life!"

"My father…?" Letty said slowly. "Is dying?"

Mrs. Pollifax's expression changed. "You didn't know?"

Shocked, she shook her head. "There must… must be some mistake. My father's not sick. He's fine. He's living without a care in the world…going to the park every day to play chess…"

"Oh, my dear." Coming closer, the housekeeper gently put her hand on Letty's shoulder. "I'm sorry. I judged you wrongly. I thought you knew. He collapsed a few weeks ago and has been in the hospital ever since. When I visited him yesterday, he didn't look well. He might have only weeks left. Days."

A loud rushing sound went through Letty's ears.

"No," she said numbly. "It has to be a mistake."

"I'm so sorry."

"You're wrong." Shaking off the housekeeper's hand, Letty reached for her phone. She dialed Darius's number first. When it went to voice mail, she hung up.

She took a deep breath. Her hands shook as she

deliberately broke her vow to her husband for the first time. Her father had always hated cell phones, disparaging them as "tracking devices," so she called him at their old apartment number.

That, too, went to voice mail. But it was no longer Letty's voice on the phone greeting. Her father had replaced it with his own. For the first time in two months, she heard his recorded voice, and it sounded different. Fragile. Weak.

Terror rushed through her.

Her body was shaking as she looked up at Mrs. Pollifax. "Which hospital?"

The housekeeper told her. "But you're in no fit state to drive. I'll have Collins bring around the car. Shall I come with you?"

Letty shook her head numbly.

The older woman bit her lip, looking sad. "He's in room 302."

The drive to Brooklyn seemed to take forever. When they finally arrived at the large, modern hospital, Letty's body shook as she raced inside.

She didn't stop at reception, just hurried to the elevator, holding her heavy, aching belly. On the third floor, she followed the signs toward room 302.

Her steps slowed when she saw a man sitting in the waiting area. He looked up and saw her, too. She frowned. She recognized him from somewhere…

But she didn't stop, just headed straight for her father's room.

"Miss!" a nurse called anxiously as she passed the third-floor reception desk, barreling toward the corner room. "Please wait just a moment."

"It's all right," Letty said. "I'm his daughter." She pushed open the door. "Dad. Dad! I'm—"

But the room was empty.

Letty stared around in shock. Was she in the wrong room? Had she misunderstood?

Was he—oh, God—surely he couldn't be...?

"I'm sorry," a woman said behind her.

"You should be!" her father's gruff voice retorted.

With a sob, Letty whirled around.

In the doorway her living, breathing father was sitting in a wheelchair, glaring back at the dark-haired nurse struggling to push him through the doorway.

"You practically ran me into a wall. Where'd you learn how to drive?"

Letty burst into noisy tears. Her father turned his head and saw her, and his gaunt, pale features lit up with joy.

"Letty. You came."

Throwing her arms around his thin frame in the wheelchair, she choked out, "Of course I came. As soon as I heard you were sick. Then when I didn't see you in the bed, I thought..."

"Oh, you thought I was dead? No!" Glancing back at the nurse, he added drily, "Not for *some* people's lack of trying."

"Hmph." The nurse sniffed. "That's the last time I agree to help you win a wheelchair race, Howard."

"Win! We didn't win anything! Margery crushed us by a full ten seconds, in spite of her extra pounds. After all my big talk, too—I'll never live this down," he complained.

Letty drew back with astonishment. "Wheelchair race?"

"Admittedly not one of my best ideas, especially with Nurse Crashy here."

"Hey!"

"But it's what passes for fun here in the hospice wing. Either that or depress myself with cable news."

"It's totally against hospital protocol. I can't believe you talked me into it. Ask someone else to risk their job next time," the nurse said.

He gave her his old charming grin. "The race was a good thing. It lifted the spirits of everyone on the wing."

Looking slightly mollified, she sighed. "I guess I'd better go try convince my boss of that." She left the room.

Her father turned back to Letty. "But why are you crying? You really thought I was dead?"

She tried to smile. "You're crying, too, Dad."

"Am I?" Her father touched his face. He gave her a watery smile. "I'm just glad to see you, I guess. I was starting to wonder if you'd ever come."

"I came the instant I heard," she whispered, feeling awful and guilty.

Howard gave a satisfied nod. "I knew he'd eventually tell you."

"Who?"

"Darius. Sure, I promised I'd never contact you. But there was nothing in our deal that said I couldn't contact *him*. I left him a message four weeks ago, when I woke up in the hospital. I'd collapsed in the street, so an ambulance brought me here."

Four weeks? Letty was numb with shock. Darius had known for a *month* that her father was in the hospital, just an hour away from Fairholme?

Her father stroked his wispy chin. "Though I'm pretty sure he knew even before that. He's had me followed since the day you ran off with him. The guy must have noticed me going to my doctor's office three times a week."

She sucked in her breath, covering her mouth. Not just one month, but two? Darius had known her father was sick, dying, but he'd purposefully kept it from her?

Your father is spending his days playing chess with friends down at the park.

A lie!

Last night, when she and Darius had been cuddled by the fire, dreaming about their child, even then, her husband had been lying to her. While Letty had been eating cookies and drinking tea, her father had been spending yet another night in this hospital. Alone. Without a single word of love from his only daughter.

A cold sweat broke out on her skin. She trembled as if to fight someone or flee. But there was no escaping the horrible truth.

Darius had lied to her.

The man she'd loved since childhood. The center of all her romantic dreams and longings. He'd known her father was dying, and he'd lied.

How could Darius have been so callous? So selfish, heartless and cruel?

The answer was obvious.

He didn't love her.

He never would.

A gasp of anguish and rage came from the back of her throat.

"He never gave you the message, did he?" her father said, watching her. When she shook her head, he sighed. "How did you know I was here?"

"Mrs. Pollifax."

"I see." He looked sad. Then his eyes fell to her belly and he brightened as he changed the subject. "You're so big! You're just a week or two from your due date, aren't you?"

"Yes."

"I've almost made it." His voice was smug. "The doctors said I was a goner, but I told them I wasn't going anyplace yet."

Letty's body was still shaking with grief and

fury. In the gray light of the hospital room, she turned toward the window. Outside, she saw November rain falling on the East River, and beyond it she could see the skyscrapers of Manhattan. Where Darius was right now.

Howard said dreamily behind her, "I was determined to see my grandbaby before I died."

She whirled back to her father. "Stop talking about dying!"

His gaunt face sagged. "I'm sorry, Letty. I really am."

"Isn't there any hope?" Her voice cracked. "An operation? A—a second opinion?"

Her father's eyes were kind. He shook his head. "I knew I was dying before I left prison."

She staggered back. "Why didn't you tell me?"

He rubbed his watery eyes. "I should have, I guess. But I didn't want you to worry and take all the stress on yourself like you always do. I wanted, for once, to take care of you. I wanted to repair the harm I did so long ago and get you back where you deserved to be. Married to your true love."

True love, Letty thought bitterly. Her stomach churned every time she thought of Darius lying to her all this time. The unfeeling bastard.

"It was my only goal," her father said. "To make sure you'd be looked after and loved after I was gone. Now you and Darius are married, expecting a baby." He grinned with his old verve and said proudly, "Getting my arm broken by that thug was the best thing that ever happened to me, since it helped me bring you back together. I can die at peace. A happy man."

"Darius never told me you were sick," she choked out, her throat aching with pain. "I'll never forgive him."

Her father's expression changed. "Don't blame Darius. After all my self-made disasters, it just shows his good sense. Shows me he'll protect you better than I ever did." He looked up from the wheelchair. "Thank you, Letty."

She felt like the worst daughter in the world. "For what?"

"For always believing in me," he said softly, "even when you had no reason to. For loving me through everything."

She looked at her dying father through her tears. Then looked around the hospital room at the plain bed, the tile floor, the antiseptic feel, the ugly medical equipment. She couldn't bear to think of him spending his last days here, whiling away his hours with wheelchair races.

Her eyes narrowed. "Do you really need to be in the hospital?"

Howard shrugged. "I could have gone to full hospice. Other than pain meds, there's not much the doctors can do for me."

Her belly tightened with a contraction that felt like nothing compared to the agony of her heart.

She lifted her chin. "Then you're coming home with me."

Howard looked at her in disbelief. "Back to that apartment? No, thanks. At least the hospital isn't cold all the time and someone brings me meals..."

"Not the apartment. I'm taking you to Fairholme."

His eyes looked dazzled.

"Fairholme?" he breathed. She saw the joy in his wrinkled face. Then he blinked, looking troubled. "But Darius—"

"I'll handle him." Wrapping her arms around her father's thin shoulders, she kissed the wispy top of his head. Her father's last days would be happy ones, she vowed. He would die in the home that he'd adored, where he'd once lived with his beloved wife and raised his child, surrounded by comfort and love.

Letty would take care of him as he'd once taken care of her.

And, she thought grimly, she'd also take care of Darius.

She'd loved her husband with all her heart. Now she saw that all the sacrifices she'd made, all of her trust, had been for nothing. For an illusion. Darius didn't love her. He would never love her.

It was his final betrayal. And for this, she would never forgive him.

Darius walked into his office near Battery Park with a smile on his face and a spring in his step. He was late but had an excellent reason. He'd stopped at his favorite jeweler's on Fifth Avenue to buy a push present for his wife.

He'd read about push presents in a parenthood article. It was a gift that men gave the mothers of their children after labor and delivery, in celebration and appreciation of all their hours of pain and hard work. Since Letty's due date was so close, Darius had known he had no time to lose. He'd found the perfect gift—exquisite emerald earrings, surrounded by diamonds, set in gold, almost as beautiful as her hazel eyes. They'd even once belonged to a queen of France. With Letty's love of history, he knew she'd get a kick out of that, and he could hardly wait to give them to her. And even more amazing: when he did, their son would be real at last, and in their arms.

Darius realized he was whistling the same hokey lullaby that his wife had sung in the shower that morning to their unborn baby.

He loved Letty's voice.

He loved their home.

And he loved that he'd been able to blow off half a morning of work in order to get her a gift. It was supposedly one of the perks of being a boss, but at his last company, he'd been too grimly driven to do anything but grind out work. So he could build his fortune. So he could be worth something.

But even after he'd succeeded, even when he'd finally been rich beyond imagination, he'd been unhappy. He realized that now. He'd spent ten years doing nothing but work, and when he'd sold his company he'd felt lost. Money hadn't fulfilled him quite as much as he'd thought it would.

But now, everything had changed. Both in his work and his life.

He was building a new company. A free website would teach software coding, math and science skills, so others could have the opportunities he'd had, to get good jobs or perhaps even start their own tech companies someday.

His goal wasn't to build a fortune. He already had more than he could spend in a lifetime. When he'd paid out billions of dollars to Howard Spencer's victims, he hadn't even missed it.

Letty was teaching him—reminding him?— how a good life was lived.

Throughout their marriage, as Fairholme had every day become more beautiful, so had his pregnant wife. She was huge now, and she glowed. Every day she told him how much she loved him. He could feel it, her love for him, warming him like a fire in winter.

There was only one flaw.

One secret he was keeping.

And he knew it might ruin everything.

Darius's steps slowed as he crossed through the open office with the exposed brick walls.

Letty's father was dying. And Darius didn't know how to tell her.

He hadn't wanted to believe it was true at first. For weeks, he'd insisted it was all an elaborate con. "Call me when he's dead," he'd told his investigator half-seriously.

Then he'd gotten a message from Howard Spencer himself, saying he was in the hospital. Even then, for a few days, Darius had told himself it was a lie. Until his investigator had combed through the hospital records and confirmed it was true. Darius had no choice but to face it.

Now he had to tell Letty.

But how? How could he explain to her all his weeks of silence, when he'd known her father was dying in a Brooklyn hospital?

Darius still believed he'd done the right thing. He and Letty had made a deal at the start of their marriage: no contact with her father. There hadn't been any fine print or "get out of jail free" card if the man decided to die. All Darius had done was uphold their deal. He had nothing to feel guilty about. He hadn't just paid Spencer's debts, but also his living expenses and even his medical bills. He'd practically acted like a saint.

Somehow, he didn't think Letty would see it that way.

Darius dreaded her reaction. He'd halfheartedly started to tell her last night, but stopped, telling himself he didn't want to risk raising her blood pressure when she was so close to delivery. He didn't want to risk her health, or the baby's.

After the baby's born, he promised himself firmly. Once he knew both mother and baby were safe and sound.

She would be angry at first, he knew. But after she'd had some time to think it over, she'd realize that he'd only been trying to protect her. And it was in her nature to forgive. She had no choice. She loved him.

Feeling calmer, he walked past his executive assistant's desk toward his private office. "Good morning, Mildred."

Lifting her eyebrows, she greeted him with "Your wife is on the line."

"My wife?" A smile lifted unbidden to his face, as it always did when he thought of Letty.

"She said you weren't answering your cell."

Instinctively, Darius put his hand to his trouser pocket. It was empty. He must have left it in the car.

"Mrs. Kyrillos sounds pretty stressed." His executive assistant, usually stern and no-nonsense, gave him a rare smile. "She said it's urgent."

Letty never called him at work. His smile changed to a dazed grin. There could be only one reason she'd call now, so close to her due date!

"I'll take it in my office," he said joyfully and rushed inside, shutting the door behind him. He snatched up the phone. "Letty? Is it the baby? Are you in labor?"

His wife's voice sounded strangely flat. "No."

"Mildred said it was urgent—"

"It is urgent. I'm leaving you. I'm filing for divorce."

For a long moment he just gripped the phone, that foolish grin still on his face, as he tried to comprehend her words. Then the smile fell away.

"What are you talking about? Is this some kind of joke?"

"No."

He took a deep breath. "I've read about pregnancy hormones…"

Anger suddenly swelled from the other end of the line.

"Pregnancy hormones? *Pregnancy hormones?* I'm divorcing you because you lied to me. You've been lying for months! My father is dying and you never told me!"

Darius's heart was suddenly in his throat.

"How did you find out?" he whispered.

"Mrs. Pollifax couldn't understand how I could be such a heartless daughter to just let my father die alone. Don't worry. I've let her know that the heartless one is you."

He looked up, past his desk to the window overlooking the southern tip of Manhattan, and the Atlantic beyond it. Outside, rain fell in the gray November morning.

He licked his lips and tried, "Letty, I don't blame you for being upset—"

"Upset? No. I'm not upset." She paused. "I'm happy."

That was so obviously not true he had no idea how to react. "If you'll just give me a chance to explain."

"You already explained to me, long ago, that you wouldn't love me. That love was for children. You told me. I just didn't listen," she said softly. "Now I really, truly get it. And I want you out of my life for good."

"No—"

"I've brought my father to Fairholme."

Gripping the phone, he nearly staggered back. "Howard Spencer—in my house?"

"Yes." Her voice was ice-cold. "I'm not leaving him in the hospital, surrounded by strangers. He's going to spend his last days surrounded by love, in the home where he was married to my mother."

"It's not just your decision. I bought that house and…" He stopped himself, realizing how pompous he sounded. But it was too late.

"Right." Her voice was a sneer. "Because money makes the man. You think you can buy your way through life. That's what you do, isn't it? Buy things. You bought my virginity, and ever since, you've kept buying me. With marriage. With money. You didn't realize it was never your money I wanted." Her voice suddenly broke to a whisper. "It was you, Darius. My dream of you. The amazing boy you were." She took a breath. "The man I actually thought you still were, deep down inside."

"I'm still that man," he said tightly. "I was going to tell you. I just didn't want you upset…"

"Upset by my father dying!"

Darius flinched at the derision in her voice. "Perhaps I made a bad decision, but I was trying to look after you."

"And you assumed I would forgive you."

He felt shaken. "Forgiveness is what you do."

She gave a hard laugh. "How convenient for you. Only the idiots who love you have to forgive. But since you never love anyone, you never have to worry about that. You're free to hurt whomever you please."

She didn't sound like his wife at all, the kind-hearted woman who greeted him every day with kisses, who gave so much of herself and asked for very little in return.

Except for him to forgive her father, Darius realized. That was the one thing she'd actually asked for. And the one thing he'd refused, again and again.

He, who was never afraid of anything, felt the first stirrings of real fear. "If you'll just listen to me—"

"I've had suitcases boxed up for you. Collins is taking them to your penthouse in Midtown. Don't worry. I won't stay here forever. You can have Fairholme back after…" Her voice was suddenly unsteady. "After. I don't want anything from you in our divorce. The baby and I will be leaving New York."

"You can't be serious."

"Poppy Alexander lives in Los Angeles now. She offered me a job a while back. I told her no. Now I'm going to say yes."

"No."

"Try and stop me. Just try." He could hear the ragged gasp of her breath. "You called my dad a monster. You're the real monster, Darius. Because you know what it was like to have your father die alone. That was the reason for all your vengeance and rage, wasn't it? That was the big reason you wouldn't let me see my dad. Well, you know what? My dad nearly died alone, too. Because of you."

The pang of fear became sharper, piercing down his spine. He licked his lips. "Letty—"

"Stay away from us," she said in a low voice. "I never want to see you again. Better that our son has no father at all than a heartless one like you."

The line went dead. He stared down at the phone in his hand.

Numb with shock, Darius raised his head. He looked blankly around his office, still decorated with his wife's sweet touches. A photo of them on their Greek honeymoon. A sonogram picture of their baby. He stared in bewilderment at the bright blue jeweler's bag on his desk. The push present for his wife, the emerald earrings once owned by a queen that he'd bought to express his appreciation and joy.

Above him, he could hear the rain falling heavily against the roof. Loud. Like a child's rattle.

And felt totally alone.

He'd known this would happen. Known if he ever lowered his guard and let himself care, he would get kicked in the teeth. Teeth? He felt like his guts had just been ripped out. For a second, he felt only that physical pain, like the flash of lightning before thunder.

Then the emotional impact reached his heart, and he had to lean one hand on his desk to keep his balance. The pain he felt then was almost more than he could bear.

Standing in his office, in the place he'd been happily whistling a lullaby just moments before, anguish and rage rushed through him. Throwing out his arm, he savagely knocked the jewelry bag to the ground.

Suddenly, he could almost understand why Howard Spencer had turned criminal when he'd lost his wife. Because Darius suddenly wanted to set fire to everything in his life, to burn it all down.

Slowly, as if he'd gained fifty years, he walked out of his office.

"Everything all right, sir?" Mildred Harrison said serenely from her desk. "Are you headed to the hospital for Mrs. Kyrillos?"

Mrs. Kyrillos. He almost laughed at the name.

She'd never been his wife, not really. How could she, when she'd seen through him from the start?

You always said a man could be measured by his money.

He looked slowly around the bustling office loft, with its exposed brick walls, its high ceilings, the open spaces full of employees busily working on computers or taking their breaks at the foosball table. He said softly, "No."

His executive assistant frowned. "Sir?"

"I don't want it anymore." Darius looked at her. "Take the company. You can have it. I'm done."

And he left without looking back.

He spent the afternoon in one of Manhattan's old dive bars, trying to get drunk. He could have called Santiago Velazquez or Kassius Black, but they weren't exactly the kind of friends who shared confidences and feelings. Darius had only really done that with Letty. He told himself Scotch would keep him company now.

It didn't.

Finally he gave up. He was alone. He would always be alone. Time to accept it.

Dropped off by the taxi, Darius came home late that night to his dark penthouse. All the bright lights of Manhattan sparkled through the floor-to-ceiling windows. He saw nothing but darkness and shadows.

And three expensive suitcases left in his foyer. Suitcases Letty had packed for him when she'd taken his measure, found him completely lacking and tossed him out of their family home.

You think you can buy your way through life. That's what you do, isn't it? Buy things.

Slowly, Darius looked around the stark, impersonal penthouse at the sparse, expensive furniture. Everything was black and white. He'd bought this place two years ago, as a trophy to show how far he'd come from the poverty-stricken village boy he'd once been. A trophy to prove to himself that Letitia Spencer had made a fatal error the day she'd decided he wasn't good enough to marry.

This penthouse was not his home.

His home was Fairholme.

Darius closed his eyes, thinking of the windswept oceanfront manor with its wide windows over the Great South Bay and the Atlantic beyond. The roses, fields and beach. The sun-drenched meadow where he'd taught Letty to dance. Where he'd first learned to love.

Letty.

He opened his eyes with a slow intake of breath.

Letty was his home.

Even during their brief marriage, he'd experienced happiness he'd never known before. The comfort and love of having a wife who put him first, who waited for him every night, who kissed him with such passion. Who slept warm and willing beside him every night in bed.

More than that. She'd reminded him who he'd once been.

You didn't realize it was never your money I wanted. It was you, Darius. My dream of you. The amazing boy you were. The man I actually thought you still were, deep down inside.

Numbly, he looked out the two-story-high windows that overlooked the twinkling lights of the city.

Letty was always determined to protect those she loved. Now she was trying to protect their child from him. Just as he'd once tried to protect Letty from her father.

You called my dad a monster. You're the real monster.

He leaned his forehead against the cold window glass.

Howard Spencer had been a good man once. He'd been a good employer to Darius's father and kind to everyone, including the scared eleven-year-old boy newly arrived from Greece. Then he'd changed after he'd lost his beloved wife.

What was Darius's excuse?

He took a deep breath, looking out bleakly into the night. Why had he been so determined to wreak vengeance on her father? So determined that he hadn't even cared how badly it might hurt Letty as collateral damage?

He should have told her the truth from the start. He should have taken her in his arms. He should have fallen to his knees. He should have told her he was sorry, and that he'd do whatever it took to make it right.

Why hadn't he?

What the hell was wrong with him?

Darius had convinced himself he was justified for his actions, because he blamed Howard Spencer for his father's early, unhappy death.

Letty was right. He was a liar. And he'd lied to himself worst of all.

The truth was, deep in his heart, there had always been only one person Darius truly blamed for his father's death, and it had been too painful for him to face till now.

Himself.

He closed his eyes as a memory that he'd pushed away for over a decade pummeled him. But today, he could no longer resist the waves of guilt and shame as he remembered.

Eugenios had called Darius in the middle of the day.

"I've lost everything, son." His Greek father, usually so distant and gruff, had sounded lost, bewildered. "I just got a certified letter. It says all my life savings—everything I invested with Mr. Spencer—it's all gone."

Darius had been busy working in his first rented office, a windowless Manhattan basement. He'd only gotten three hours of sleep the night before. It was the first time the two men had talked in months, since Letty had dumped him and caused Eugenios to be fired and tossed from Fairholme. Just hearing his voice that day had reminded Darius of everything he was trying so hard to forget. A lifetime of resentment had exploded.

"I guess that pays you back for all your loyalty to Spencer, huh, Dad? All those years when you put him first, even over your own family."

Darius had been so young, so self-righteous. It made him feel sick now to remember it.

"That was my job." His father's voice had trembled. "I wanted to make sure I never lost a job again. Never felt again like I did that awful day we found you on the doorstep…"

The awful day they found him? Darius's hurt and anger blocked out the rest of his father's words as Eugenios continued feebly, "I had no money. No job. I couldn't let my family starve. You don't know what that does to a man, to have nothing…"

It was the most his father had ever spoken to him. And Darius's cold reply had haunted him ever since.

"So you had nothing then, huh, Dad? Well, guess what? You have nothing now. You ignored me my whole childhood for nothing. You have nothing. You *are* nothing."

He'd hung up the phone.

An hour later, his father had quietly died of a heart attack in his Queens apartment, sinking to his kitchen floor, where he was found later by a neighbor.

Darius's hands tightened to fists against the window.

His father had never been demonstrative. In Darius's childhood, there had been no hugs and very little praise. Even the attention of criticism was rare.

But Darius and his grandmother hadn't starved. Eugenios had provided for them. He'd taught his work ethic by example. He'd worked hard, trying to give his son a better life.

And after all his years of stoically supporting them, after he'd lost his job and money, Darius had scorned him.

Remembering it now, he felt agonizing shame.

He hadn't wanted to remember the last words he'd spoken to his proud Greek father. So instead he'd sought vengeance on Howard Spencer, carefully blaming him alone.

Darius had thought if he never loved anyone, he'd never feel pain; and if he was rich, he'd be happy.

Look at me now, he thought bitterly, surveying the elegant penthouse. Surrounded by money. And never more alone.

He missed Letty.

Craved her desperately.

He loved her.

Darius looked up in shock.

He'd never stopped loving her.

All these years, he'd tried to pretend he didn't. Tried to control her, to possess her, to pretend he didn't care. He'd hidden his love away like a coward, afraid of the pain and shame of possible loss, while Letty let her love shine for all the world to see.

He'd thought Letty weak? He took a shuddering breath. She was the strongest person he knew. She'd offered him loyalty, kindness, self-sacrifice. She'd offered him every bit of her heart and soul. And in return, he'd offered her money.

Darius clawed back his hair. She was right. He'd tried to buy her. But money didn't make the man. *Love did.*

Darius loved her. He was completely, wildly in love with Letty. He wanted to be her husband. To live with her. To raise their baby. To be happy. To be home.

His eyes narrowed.

But how? How could he show her he had more to offer? How could he convince her to forgive him?

Forgiveness. His lips twisted with the bitter irony. The very thing he'd refused to give her all these months, he would now be begging for...

But for her, he'd do anything. He set his jaw. With the same total focus he'd built his empire, he would win back his wife.

Over the next month, he tried everything.

He respected her demand that he stay away from

her, even after his friend Velazquez sent him a link to a birth announcement, and he saw his son had been safely born, weighing seven pounds and fourteen ounces. Both mother and baby were doing well.

Darius had jumped up, overwhelmed with the need to go see them in the hospital, to hold them in his arms.

But he knew bursting into her room against her express wishes would have only made things worse, not better. So he restrained himself, though it took all his self-control. He cleaned out a flower shop and sent all the flowers and toys and gifts to her maternity suite at the hospital. Anonymously.

Then he'd waited hopefully.

He'd found out later that she'd immediately forwarded all the flowers, toys and gifts straight to the sick children's ward.

Well played, he'd thought with a sigh. But he wasn't done. He'd contacted Mildred and she'd sent him via courier the jewelry bag he'd left in his office. He'd sent it to Fairholme, again anonymously.

A few days later he received a thank-you card from Mrs. Pollifax, stating that the earrings had been sold and the money donated to the housekeeper's favorite charity, an animal shelter on Long Island.

He'd ground his teeth, but doggedly kept trying. Over the next week, he sent gifts addressed to Letty. He sent a card congratulating her on the baby. On Thanksgiving, he even had ten pies from her favorite bakery delivered to her at Fairholme.

Pies she immediately forwarded to a homeless shelter.

As the rain of November changed to the snows of December, Darius's confidence started to wane. Once, in a moment of weakness, he drove by Fairholme late at night, past the closed gate.

But she was right. He couldn't even see the house.

After the pie incident, Darius gave up sending gifts. When she continued to refuse his calls, he stopped those, too. He kept writing heartfelt letters, and for a few weeks, he was hopeful, until they were all returned at once, unopened.

His baby son was now four weeks old. The thought made him sick with grief. Darius hadn't seen him. Hadn't held him. He didn't even know his name.

His wife wanted to divorce him. His son didn't have a father. Darius felt like a failure.

In the past, he would have taken his sense of grief and powerlessness and hired the most vicious, shark-infested law firm in Manhattan to punish her, to file for full custody.

But he didn't want that.

He wanted her.

He wanted his family back.

Finally, as Christmas approached, he knew he was out of ideas. He had only one card left to play.

But when he went to see his lawyer, the man's jaw dropped.

"If you do this, Mr. Kyrillos, in my opinion you're a fool."

He was right. Darius was a fool. Because this was his last desperate hope.

But was he brave enough to actually go through with it? Could he jump off that cliff, and take a gamble that would either win him back the woman he loved, or cost him literally everything?

The afternoon of Christmas Eve Darius got the package from his lawyer. He was holding it in his hands, pacing his penthouse apartment like a trapped animal when his phone rang. Lifting it from his pocket, he saw the number from Fairholme.

His heart started thudding frantically. He snatched it up so fast he almost dropped it before he placed it against his ear. "Letty?"

But it wasn't his wife. Instead, the voice on the line belonged to the last person he'd ever imagined would call him.

CHAPTER ELEVEN

"IT'S YOUR VERY first Christmas," Letty crooned to her tiny baby, walking him through Fairholme's great hall. She was already dressed for Christmas Eve dinner in a long scarlet velvet dress and soft kid leather bootees. She'd dressed her newborn son in an adorable little Santa outfit.

She'd asked Mrs. Pollifax to make all her father's holiday favorites, ham, plum pudding, potatoes, in hopes of tempting him to eat more than his usual scant bites. They'd even brought the dining table into the great hall, beside the big stone fireplace, so they could have dinner beneath the enormous Christmas tree.

Letty wanted this Christmas to be perfect. Because she knew it would be her father's last. The doctor had said yesterday that Howard's body was failing rapidly. It would likely be only days now.

Her heart twisted with grief. Her only comfort was that she'd tried her best to make his last few weeks special.

A lump rose in Letty's throat as she looked up at the two-story-high tree, decorated with sparkling lights and a mix of ornaments, old and new. Some of them Letty had treasured since childhood. And now they were back here, where they belonged. Funny to think she had Darius to thank for that. If he hadn't found her in Brooklyn and stopped her from taking that desperate bus ride out of the city, the ornaments would have been long lost to a junk dealer or the landfill.

Without him, she wouldn't be here now. Her father couldn't have come to Fairholme for his last Christmas, nor would her baby be here for his first one. It was because of Darius.

She missed him. No matter how much she denied it. No matter how she tried not to.

Every time some thoughtful gift had arrived at the house, she'd pictured how her father had looked in the hospital, so pale and alone. She'd remembered how Darius had taken her love for granted, and selfishly lied. She'd told herself she was done loving someone who could never love her back.

But as the gifts tapered off, and the phone calls stopped, and the letters stopped arriving in the mail, she hadn't felt triumphant. At all.

"I hate him," she said aloud. "I never want to see him again." She wasn't sure she sounded convincing, even to her own ears. So turning to her son, she held out one of the homemade ornaments. "Look!"

"Gah," the baby replied, waving his little hands unsteadily.

"You're so smart!" She let him feel the soft fabric of the dove against his cheek, then put it back on the tree before he tried to eat it. "Your grandma Constance made that," she said softly. "I just wish she could have met you."

Her six-week-old baby smiled back, Letty would swear he did, even though her father continued to rather annoyingly claim it was only gas. Letty knew her own baby, didn't she?

Even though Darius didn't.

The thought caused an unpleasant jolt. She'd thought she was doing the right thing to exclude him. She couldn't allow such a heartless man near her baby. Even if he *was* the father.

But Darius hadn't even laid eyes on their baby, or held him, or heard the sweet gurgle of his voice or his angry cry when he wasn't fed fast enough. Darius had already missed so much. Six weeks of sleepless nights, of exhaustion and confusion.

But also six weeks of getting to know this brand-new little person. From the moment her son had been placed in her arms at the hospital, Letty had felt her heart expand in a way she'd never known before.

Darius didn't know that feeling. He didn't know his son at all. Because of her actions.

Two weeks ago, her baby had been irritable and sleepless at midnight, so she'd wrapped him in a warm blanket and put him in the stroller to walk him up and down the long driveway, behind the gate. Then she'd seen a dark sports car driving slowly by.

Darius! She'd practically run to the gate, panting as she pushed the stroller ahead of her. But by the time she reached the gate, the car was long gone. For long moments she stared through the bars of the gate, looking bleakly down the dark, empty road, hearing only the waves crashing down on the shore. And she'd realized for the first time how empty the house felt without him, even with her father and her baby and all the household staff. She missed him.

No. I don't, she told herself desperately. And if she hadn't filed for divorce yet or hired an attorney, that was only because she just hadn't had the time. Taking care of a newborn, caring for her father and decorating for Christmas would be enough to keep anyone busy, wouldn't it?

Letty's lips twisted downward. She'd said things that would never be forgiven. She'd made her choice clear. She'd used his every olive branch as a stick to stab him with.

That car probably hadn't even been his. He'd probably moved on entirely, and if she ever heard from him again, it would be only via his lawyer, demanding custody. She stiffened at the thought.

Carrying her baby up to the nursery, she fed him, rocking him for nearly an hour in the glider until he slept and she was nearly asleep herself. She smiled down at his sweet little face. His cheeks were already growing chubby. Tucking him gently in his crib for his late afternoon nap, she turned on the baby monitor and crept out of the darkened nursery.

She closed the door softly behind her. Light from the leaded glass windows reflected against the glossy hardwood floors and oak paneling of the second-floor hallway, resting with a soft haze on an old framed family photo on the wall. She looked at her own chubby face when she'd been just a toddler with two parents beaming behind her.

Trying to ignore the ache in her throat, Letty started to turn toward the stairs. Then she heard low male voices coming from down the hall.

Her father's bedroom was the nicest and biggest, the room he'd once shared with her mother, with a view of the sea. He rarely got up from his bed anymore, except when Letty managed to cajole him into his wheelchair and take him down in the elevator for a stroll around the winter garden, or to sit in a comfortable spot near the fire, beneath the Christmas tree, as the baby lay nearby.

But the male voice Letty heard talking to her father didn't sound like Paul, his nurse. Who was it? Frowning, she drew closer.

"Yes," she heard her father say, his voice a little slurred. "Always a good kid."

"I can't believe you're saying that, after everything."

Hearing the visitor's voice, low and clear, Letty's knees went weak outside her father's door. What was Darius doing here? How had he gotten into Fairholme?

"You weren't so bad. Just prickly, like your father. Eugenios was the best employee I ever had. We used to talk about you. He loved you."

"He had a funny way of showing it." Her husband's voice wasn't bitter, just matter-of-fact.

Howard gave a laugh that ended in a wheeze. "In our generation, fathers showed love differently."

"Yet Letty always knew you loved her."

"I didn't grow up with your father's fears." Howard paused. "From the age of fifteen, he was your grandmother's sole support. When you came along, he lost any chance of a job in Greece."

"I know."

"His greatest fear was of not providing for you." Coughing a laugh, Howard added, "Maybe if I'd been a little more careful about that myself, I wouldn't have left my daughter destitute while I spent years in prison. It's only because of you that we're back home now. That's why I called. I'm grateful."

Darius's voice was suddenly urgent. "Then convince Letty to stay."

"Stay? Where would she go?"

"She says as soon as you're dead, she's leaving New York."

Howard gave a low laugh. "That sounds like her. Foolish as her old man. Can't see the love right in front of her eyes, has to flee her own happiness because she's afraid. Actually, now that I think about it, she sounds like you."

Letty's heart was pounding as she leaned against the oak-paneled wall beside the open door, holding absolutely still as she listened intently.

Silence. Then Darius said in a voice so low she almost couldn't hear, "I'm sorry I blamed you for my father's death all these years. The truth is, the person I really hated was myself. I said something terrible to my dad right before he died. I'll never forgive myself."

"Whatever it was," Howard said simply, "your father forgave you long ago. He knew you loved him. Just as he loved you. He was proud of you, Darius. And seeing that you were brave enough to come here today, I am, too."

Her father was proud of the man who'd treated her so badly, who'd lied to her? Letty sucked in her breath with an astonished little squeak.

There was a pause.

"Letty," her father said drily, "I know you're there. Come in."

Her heart was in her throat. She wanted to flee but knew she'd only look foolish and cowardly. Lifting her chin, she went into her father's room.

His bedroom was full of light from the bay window. Her father was stretched out beneath the blankets, propped up by pillows, his nightstand covered with pill bottles. His gaunt face smiled up at her weakly, his eyes glowing with love.

Then, with a deep breath, Letty looked at the man standing beside the bed.

Tall and broad-shouldered and alive, Darius seemed to radiate power. For a moment, her eyes devoured his image. He was dressed simply in a dark shirt, dark jeans. His hands lifted, then fell to his sides as he looked at her, as if he had to physically restrain himself from touching her. But his dark eyes seared her. Their heartbreak and yearning cut her to the bone.

Her body reacted involuntarily, stumbling back as her heart pounded with emotion. Fury. Regret. Longing...

"What are you doing here?" she whispered.

"He's here to meet his son," her father said.

She whirled on her father, feeling betrayed. "Dad!"

"And I want him to stay for Christmas Eve dinner," he continued calmly.

She stared at him in shock. "No!"

Her father gave her a weakened version of his old charming smile. "Surely you wouldn't refuse your dying father his last Christmas wish?"

No. Of course she couldn't. She ground her teeth. "He kept me from you for two months!"

Her father stared her down. "Only a little longer than you've kept him from his son."

"I would like to meet him," Darius said quietly. "But if you don't want me around after that, I won't stay."

Trembling, she tossed her head defiantly. "Did he tell you the baby's name?"

"No."

"It's Howard." She lifted her chin, folding her arms. "Howard Eugenios Spencer."

To her shock, Darius didn't scowl or bluster. He didn't even flinch. He just looked at her with that same strange glow of longing in his eyes.

"That's not the name I would have chosen." Triumph surged through her as she waited for him to be sarcastic and show his true colors in front of her father. Instead, he just said quietly, "His last name should be Kyrillos."

Darius was upset only about the surname? Not about the fact that she'd named their precious baby son after her father—his hated enemy?

"Aren't you furious?" she said, dropping her arms in bewilderment.

His lips curved as he looked down at her father, then slowly shook his head. "Not as much as I used to be."

Darius came toward her. It took all Letty's willpower not to step back from him as he towered over her. It wasn't him she was afraid of, but herself. Her whole body was trembling with her own longing. Her need. She missed him.

But she couldn't. She'd made her choice! She wouldn't be married to a man who didn't love her!

"Please let me see my son," he said humbly. He bowed his head, as if waiting for her verdict.

"Let him," her father said.

Looking between the two men, she knew she was outnumbered. She snapped, "Fine."

Turning on her heel, she walked out. She didn't look back to see if Darius was following her. Her hands were trembling.

All these weeks when she'd pushed him away, she'd pictured him as angry, arrogant, heartless. It was why she hadn't been tempted to open his letters—why would she, when she knew he'd only be yelling at her?

She'd never once imagined Darius looking at her the way he did now, with such heartbreaking need. But it wasn't just desire. He had an expression in his eyes that she hadn't seen since—

No! She wasn't going to let her own longing talk her into seeing things in his eyes that weren't there, things that didn't exist.

Pressing a finger to her lips, she quietly pushed open the nursery door and crept into the shadowy room, motioning for him to follow. Darius came in behind her.

Then, as they both stood over the crib, Letty made the mistake of looking at her husband when he saw their son for the very first time.

Darius's dark eyes turned fierce, almost bewildered with love when he looked at their sleeping baby. Tenderly, he reached out in the semidarkness and stroked his dark downy head as he slept.

"My son," he whispered. "My sweet boy."

A lump rose in her throat so huge it almost choked her. And she suddenly knew that Darius wasn't the only one who'd been heartless.

What had she done?

Blinded by furious grief at his lie about her father, Letty had actually kept Darius from his own firstborn son. *For six weeks.*

Anguish and regret rushed through her in a torrent of pain. Even if Darius could never love her, she had no doubt that he loved their baby. Especially as she watched him now, gently stroking their baby's small back through his Santa onesie as the sleeping child gave a soft snuffle in the shadowy room.

She'd had no right to steal his child away.

"I'm sorry," she choked out. He looked up.

"You're sorry?"

Unable to speak for misery, she nodded.

Reaching out in the shadowy nursery, beneath the hazy colors of the goose girl fresco, Darius put his hand gently on Letty's shoulder, and she shuddered beneath his touch.

"Letty...there's something you should know."

Their eyes locked, and she saw something in his black eyes that made the world tremble beneath her feet.

Panic rushed through her heart. Seeing Darius make peace with her father, seeing him look so lovingly at their baby, had cracked open her soul and everything she hadn't wanted to feel had rushed in.

She'd painted him so badly in her mind. She'd called him a monster. And yes, he never should have lied about her father.

But when she'd said horrible things and threatened to take his child permanently away, he hadn't hired some awful lawyer to fight her. He'd done what she asked, and stayed away. Obviously at great emotional cost.

Now, she saw his sensual lips part, heard his hoarse intake of breath and knew whatever he was about to say would change her life forever. He was going to tell her he was done with her. She'd won. He'd given up. Now he wanted to talk like reasonable adults about sharing custody of their son.

She'd destroyed their marriage with her anger and pride. She'd told herself she'd rather be alone than married to a man who didn't love her. Now she suddenly couldn't bear to hear him speak the words that would end it…

"No," she choked out.

Turning, she fled the nursery. She ran down the hall, down the stairs, her heart pounding, gasping for breath.

She heard him coming down after her. "Letty!"

She didn't stop. Pushing off the stairs, she ran outside, into the snow.

Her mother's rose garden was barren in winter, nothing but thorny vines and dead leaves covered in a blanket of white. Letty's soft black boots stumbled forward, her long red dress dragging behind, scarlet against the snow.

But he swiftly caught her, roughly pushing her wrists against the outside wall of the greenhouse with its flash of exotic greenery behind the steamy glass. She struggled, but he wouldn't let go.

She felt his heat. His power. She felt the strength of her own longing for this man, whom she continued to love in the face of despair.

"Let me go," she cried.

"Forgive me," Darius choked out. He lowered his head against hers. She heard the heavy gasp of his breath. "You were right, Letty. About everything. I'm so sorry."

Her lips parted. She looked up at him in shock.

"*You're* sorry?" she whispered. "I kept you from our baby."

"You were right to kick me out of your life." He cupped her face in both his hands. "I blamed you and your father for so much. I blamed everyone but the person really at fault. Myself."

"Darius—"

"No." He held up his hand. "Let me say this. I don't know if I'll get another chance."

All around them in the silent white garden, soft snow began to fall from the lowering gray clouds. Letty's heart was suddenly in her throat. Now he was going to tell her that they were better off apart...

"You're right, Letty," he said in a low voice. "I

did try to buy you. I thought money was all I had to offer anyone. I thought I could selfishly claim your love, while being cowardly enough to protect my own heart. But I failed." He gave a low laugh. "The truth is, I failed long ago."

His dark eyes had a suspicious gleam. Surely Darius Kyrillos, the ruthless Greek billionaire, couldn't have tears in his eyes? No. It must be the cold winter wind, whipping against his skin.

"I loved you, Letty. It terrified me. My whole life, all I've ever known of love is loss. Losing you all those years ago almost destroyed me. I never wanted to feel like that again. So I buried my soul in ice. Then when I saw you again, when I first took you to my bed, everything changed. Against my will, the ice cracked. But even then I was afraid." Taking a deep breath, he lifted his eyes to hers. "I'm not afraid anymore."

"You're not?" she whispered, her heart falling.

With a little smile, he shook his head. He took her hand in his larger one. "Now I know the truth is that love never ends. Not real love. The love your father has for you and my father had for me. The love your parents had for each other." His hand tightened over hers as he said softly, "And even if you divorce me, Letty, even if you never want to see me again after tonight, I can still love you. And it won't bring me pain, but joy, because of everything you've brought to my life. You saved me. Made me feel again. Taught me to love again.

Gave me a son." Stroking her cheek, he whispered, "No matter what happens, I will always be grateful. And love you."

His hand was warm over hers. With him so close, she didn't even feel the snow. Trembling, she whispered, "Darius...what are you saying?"

His jaw tightened. "If you still want to divorce me, you won't need a lawyer." He reached into his shirt pocket, where a single page was folded in quarters. "Here."

Opening the paper, she looked down at it numbly. She tried to read it, but the words jumbled together. "What's this?"

"Everything," he said quietly. "Fairholme. The jets. My stocks, bonds, bank accounts. It's all been transferred to your name. Everything I possess."

She gasped, then shook her head. "But you know money doesn't mean anything to me!"

"Yes, I know that." He looked at her. "But you know what it means to me."

Letty's eyes went wide.

Because she did know what Darius's fortune meant to him. It meant ten years of twenty-hour workdays and sleeping in basements. It meant working till he collapsed, day after day, with no time to relax or see friends. No time to even *have* friends. It meant borrowing money that he knew he'd have to pay back, even if his business failed. It meant taking terrifying risks and praying they would somehow pay off.

Those dreams had been fulfilled. Through work and will and luck, a poverty-stricken boy whose mother had abandoned him as a baby had built a multibillion-dollar empire.

This was what she now held in her hand.

"But I'm not just offering you my fortune, Letty," he said quietly. "I'm offering everything. My whole life. Everything I've been. Everything I am." Lifting her hand, he pressed it against his rough cheek and whispered, "I offer you my heart."

Letty realized she was crying.

"I love you, Letitia Spencer Kyrillos," he said hoarsely. "I know I've lost your love, your trust. But I'll do everything I can to regain your devotion. Even if it takes me a hundred years, I'll never…"

"Stop." Violently, she pushed the paper against his chest. When he wouldn't take it, it fell to the snow.

"Letty," he choked out, his dark eyes filled with misery.

"I don't want it." She lifted her hand to his scratchy cheek, rough and unshaven. Reaching her other arm around his shoulders, she whispered, "I just want you, Darius."

The joy that lit up his dark eyes was brighter than the sun.

"I don't deserve you."

"I'm not exactly perfect myself."

He immediately began protesting that she was, in fact, perfect in every way.

"It doesn't matter." Smiling, she reached up on her toes to kiss him, whispering, "We can just love each other, flaws and all."

Holding her tight, he kissed her passionately against the greenhouse, with the hot wet jungle behind the glass, as they embraced in the snow-swept bare garden. They kissed each other in a private vow that would endure all the future days of sunshine and snow, good times and bad, all the laughter and anger and pleasure and forgiveness until death.

Their love was meant to be. It was fate. *Moíra.*

They clung to each other until he broke apart with a guilty laugh.

"Ah, Letty, I'll never be perfect, that's for sure," Darius murmured, smiling down at her through his tears. "But there's one thing you should know…" Cupping her cheek, lightly drawing away the cold wet tendrils of her hair that had stuck to her skin, he whispered, "For you, I intend to spend the rest of my life trying."

Spring came early to Fairholme.

Darius had a bounce in his step as he came into the house that afternoon with a bouquet of flowers. He'd had to work on a Saturday because it was crunch time developing the new website. But he was hoping the flowers would make her forgive the fact that he'd missed their new Saturday morning family tradition of waffles and bacon.

Darius had started that tradition himself, in the weeks he'd taken to focus only on Letty and their beloved son, whom they'd nicknamed Howie. After that, encouraged by Letty, he'd sheepishly called Mildred and apologized, then asked if there was any way she could try to reassemble his team at the office.

"The office is still in fine fettle," she'd replied crisply. "I've been running everything just as you requested. I knew whatever you were going through you'd soon come to your senses. I haven't worked for you all these years for nothing."

He choked out a laugh, then said with real gratitude, "What would I do without you?"

"You'll find out next summer," she'd said firmly, "when you send my husband and me on a four-week first-class cruise through Asia. It's already booked."

Darius grinned to himself, remembering. He was grateful to Mildred. Grateful to all the people around him, his employees and most of all his family, who saw through all his flaws but were somehow willing to put up with him anyway.

Money didn't make the man. He knew that now. What made a man was what he did with his life. With his time. With his heart.

His father-in-law had died in January, surrounded by family, with a smile on his drawn face. Right before he died, his eyes suddenly glowed with joy as he breathed, "Oh. There you are…"

"He saw my mother before he died," Letty told Darius afterward, her beautiful face sparkling with tears. "How can I even be sad, when I know they're together?"

Darius wasn't so sure, but who was he to say? Love could work miracles. He was living proof of that.

Now he looked around his home with deep contentment. The oak floors gleamed and fresh-cut flowers from the greenhouse filled all the vases.

Fairholme was about to be invaded by more of the Kyrillos family. He'd sent his private plane to Heraklios, and tomorrow, Theia Ioanna, along with a few cousins, would arrive for a monthlong visit. His great-aunt's desire to meet her great-great-nephew had finally overcome her fear of flying.

He relished the thought of having his extended family here. Heaven knew Fairholme had plenty of room.

Love was everywhere. Love was everything. His son was only five months old, but he'd already collected toys from all the people who loved him around the globe. His wife did that, he thought. With her great heart, she brought everyone together with her kindness and loyalty. She was the center of Darius's world.

"Letty!" he called, holding the flowers tightly.

"She's outside, Mr. Kyrillos," the housekeeper called from the kitchen. "The weather's so fine, she and the baby went for a picnic in the meadow."

Dropping his computer bag, he went outside, past the garden, where even though the air was cool beneath the sunshine, tulips and daffodils were starting to bloom. He walked the path through the softly waving grass until he reached the meadow where he'd first taught his wife to dance. Where she'd first taught him to dream.

He stopped.

The sky was a vivid blue, the meadow the rich gold-green of spring, and in the distance, he could see the ocean. He saw Letty's beautiful face, alight with joy, as she sang their five-month-old baby a song in Greek, swinging him gently in her arms as he giggled and shrieked with happiness. Behind them on the hillside, a blanket was covered with a picnic basket, teething toys and that well-worn book about the bunny rabbit. But now, as always, Letty was dancing. Letty was singing.

Letty was love.

Darius stared at them, and for a moment the image caught at his heart, as he wondered what he'd ever done to deserve such happiness.

Then, quickening his steps, he raced to join them.

* * * * *

If you enjoyed this story, take a look at
Jennie Lucas's other great reads!
BABY OF HIS REVENGE
A RING FOR VINCENZO'S HEIR
Available now!

Also look out for more
ONE NIGHT WITH CONSEQUENCES *stories*
A CHILD CLAIMED BY GOLD
by Rachael Thomas
THE GUARDIAN'S VIRGIN WARD
by Caitlin Crews
CLAIMING HIS CHRISTMAS CONSEQUENCE
by Michelle Smart
Available now!